"Would you like a nightcap?" Lucas asked Rosie.

"Wine's fine. A small one." What the heck. She was having a good time with Lucas, the most wonderful man she'd known. He'd been there for her all day, had shared the fun and laughter with a complete group of strangers. And he was so handsome her mouth watered looking at him.

"How does it feel to see your brother so happy?"

"I'm thrilled."

Out on the deck, Lucas leaned against the railing. Rosie joined him, letting her shoulder touch his lightly, hoping he wouldn't move away. He didn't; instead he leaned in closer. Did he want more, too?

Rosie turned to put her glass down on the tiny table. To hell with this. Sometimes a person had to take risks, chance their feelings.

It felt like this was her moment.

T0357606

Dear Reader,

Rosie and Lucas's story is my 50th Harlequin Medical Romance book, and it's been as much fun writing their love story as it was with the couple in my first Medical Romance novel.

When Lucas lost his wife in an accident, he believed he'd lost everything, until he was reacquainted with Rosie, a friend from the past. She starts to wake him up to the possibility of love, which is downright scary.

That is, if Rosie can get past her own belief that she's unlovable. She never allows a man in too close for fear of being let down, so she can't understand why Lucas is making her feel special. Instinctively, she's on guard, protecting her heart, but how long can she hold out?

Enjoy following Rosie and Lucas as they fight their demons to find true happiness.

All the best,

Sue MacKay

WEDDING DATE WITH THE ER DOCTOR

SUE MacKAY

MEDICAL ROMANCE

If you purchased this book without a cover you should be aware that this book is stolen property. It was reported as "unsold and destroyed" to the publisher, and neither the author nor the publisher has received any payment for this "stripped book."

MEDICAL ROMANCE

ISBN-13: 978-1-335-94295-1

Wedding Date with the ER Doctor

Copyright © 2025 by Sue MacKay

All rights reserved. No part of this book may be used or reproduced in any manner whatsoever without written permission.

Without limiting the author's and publisher's exclusive rights, any unauthorized use of this publication to train generative artificial intelligence (AI) technologies is expressly prohibited.

This is a work of fiction. Names, characters, places and incidents are either the product of the author's imagination or are used fictitiously. Any resemblance to actual persons, living or dead, businesses, companies, events or locales is entirely coincidental.

For questions and comments about the quality of this book, please contact us at CustomerService@Harlequin.com.

TM and ® are trademarks of Harlequin Enterprises ULC.

Harlequin Enterprises ULC
22 Adelaide St. West, 41st Floor
Toronto, Ontario M5H 4E3, Canada
www.Harlequin.com

Printed in U.S.A.

Recycling programs
for this product may
not exist in your area.

Sue MacKay lives with her husband in New Zealand's beautiful Marlborough Sounds, with the water on her doorstep and the birds and the trees at her back door. It's the perfect setting to indulge her passions of entertaining friends by cooking them sumptuous meals, drinking fabulous wine, going for hill walks or kayaking around the bay—and, of course, writing stories.

Books by Sue MacKay

Harlequin Medical Romance

Queenstown Search & Rescue

Captivated by Her Runaway Doc
A Single Dad to Rescue Her
From Best Friends to I Do?

Stranded with the Paramedic
Single Mom's New Year Wish
Brought Together by a Pup
Fake Fiancée to Forever?
Resisting the Pregnant Pediatrician
Marriage Reunion with the Island Doc
Paramedic's Fling to Forever
Healing the Single Dad Surgeon
Brooding Vet for the Wallflower

Visit the Author Profile page
at Harlequin.com for more titles.

To Lindsay, without your unfailing support, book No. 50 would've been a lot harder to achieve. Love you.

And to HM&B editors who've also supported me on this amazing journey to reach 50. You're all amazing.

And to the Blenheim, NZ, police for helping me at an awful time.

**Praise for
Sue MacKay**

"Ms. MacKay has delivered a really good read in this book where the chemistry between this couple was strong; the romance was delightful and had me loving how these two come together."

—*Harlequin Junkie* on
The Italian Surgeon's Secret Baby

CHAPTER ONE

'THANK GOODNESS THAT'S DONE.'

Rosie Carter shoved the trolley containing a week's worth of groceries out through the main door of the supermarket and headed for her car. After three long and involved pickups of seriously injured people on the rescue chopper she was ready for a hot shower, followed by dinner without any interruptions on the deck at her apartment.

Melbourne had turned on the best late-summer weather imaginable. A cloudless blue sky, still air and a bearable temperature, which made wearing all the high-vis gear required on the job a bit more comfortable. No bumpy rides today, not that they often bothered her. She loved flying, whether in a chopper or a plane. So much so she was contemplating learning to fly and getting her private pilot's licence. She should stop dithering and sign up for lessons, except there was never much spare time in her life. Whenever she took on a project she gave it her all, otherwise what was the point?

At the car, Rosie pinged the locks and lifted the boot lid to stow her grocery bags.

Vroom. The sound of a speeding vehicle reached her, sounding very close. *Vroom.*

Spinning around, she heard tyres squeal to a stop right beside her. A wide-eyed man stared at her through the open window of a car.

'What the—?'

A hand shot out towards her, snatched her handbag from over her shoulder and pulled hard.

Instinctively, Rosie grabbed at it, touching it briefly before he threw it onto the seat beside him. Shoving her arm through the open window in an attempt to get her bag back, her hand slammed into the man's chest.

He punched her upper arm hard, then spun the car away, sending her crashing onto the asphalt.

Intuitively, Rosie did a three-sixty roll away from danger and came up hard against the back of her car. Immediately she leapt to her feet, feeling endangered and looking for her attacker.

He'd gone. The car sped through the car park, dangerously close to other people and vehicles. He drove straight through the stop sign and across the centre of the roundabout before disappearing out of sight.

People were rushing to her aid. 'Hey, lady, are you all right?'

'Take it easy. You might be injured.'

'I can't believe what he just did!'

Her head pounded and pain tore through her right hip and thigh. Rosie sagged against the side of her car, shaking from top to toe. 'What the hell?'

'Here, sit down before you fall again.' A man took her elbow and opened the back door so she could collapse on the edge of the seat.

'Th-thanks.' What was that about?

A young woman approached. 'I've called the police. They're on their way. So is an ambulance.'

She didn't need that. She was an emergency doctor. She could take care of herself. But she wasn't getting a word in as everyone yabbered on about what they'd seen. Drawing in a breath, Rosie concentrated on her body, wondering what damage had been done. She was hurting but nothing felt broken even though she had impacted damned hard with the ground. Her forehead had also taken a blow against the back wheel but she'd be fine to go home after she talked to the cops. There was no way she wasn't waiting to tell them the little she'd actually seen.

'I'll go over to the supermarket and see if they've got CCTV,' said the man who'd helped her onto the back seat. 'They should do, but who knows these days? They're not always working properly.'

'I saw it happen,' another man said. 'It was lucky no one else was hit by the car as it sped away.'

'I chased after him, which was plain stupid as he was in one hell of a hurry to get away,' another man said with a wry smile. 'What I thought I'd do if I did get him, I have no idea.'

'Glad you didn't reach him,' Rosie said. She didn't want anyone else hurt by that creep. Her head throbbed so hard it felt as though it was going to split in half. 'Like me trying to grab back my bag.'

'You had a wallet in there?' asked the woman who'd called the cops.

If she'd had the energy she'd have sworn. 'My credit cards need cancelling.' She stood up. Her head spun.

'Is there someone you can call to do that?'

No partner to sort this out. No one who had her bank details either. No phone to call the banks with. Her head spun harder. This was one time it would be great not to have closed herself off from men when they'd got too close. But protecting her heart was far more important than having someone to help her through the next few hours.

Someone caught her arm. 'Steady.'

'Cops are here.'

Rosie tried to straighten up, but it hurt too much everywhere. Looking around, she saw one policewoman walking towards her with a grim expression on her face while another was already talking to one of the men who'd witnessed what happened.

'Hello there. I'm Megan Harris from the local station. How are you feeling?'

A bunch of roses. 'I'm okay. Sore, but angry more than anything. I don't know…' The words stopped as her vision blurred briefly. Great. She really wasn't as all together as she'd hoped. Sinking back onto the seat, she said with as much confidence as she could manage, 'I'm Rosie Carter.'

'Right, Rosie. My colleague is going to take short statements from those who saw what happened. Another has gone to see if the CCTV picked up anything. I'd like you to tell me what you can. Can you manage that?'

'Of course I can,' she snapped, then instantly felt bad. This woman was on her side. She wasn't the enemy. 'Sorry. I'd like to get this done and then I can head home.'

'You're not going anywhere until the ambulance crew have checked you out, and then most likely it'll be a trip to the emergency department for a thorough going-over.' Megan smiled sympathetically. 'I know it's the last place you want to be right now, but they'll have to take you because once they're called they can't leave you. Unless you sign a document releasing them, that is.'

Rosie started to nod and immediately regretted it as the pounding in her head intensified. 'I'm an emergency doctor on the choppers.'

'Then you'll be familiar with the process. Right, fill me in as best you can.'

'It all happened so fast. I don't know a lot.' How embarrassing.

'Not uncommon.'

'I hit him when I tried to get my bag back. I have no idea why I did that.' But at least she had tried and not let the creep think she was a pushover.

'It would've been a reflex reaction and there's not a lot you can do about those. Did you get a good look at his face?'

She shuddered. 'Wide staring eyes that suggested he was drugged to the hilt.' She'd seen it enough when working in emergency departments to know. 'But I doubt I could pick him out in a line-up. Not with certainty anyway.'

'At least you're honest. Better to hear that than be led up the path by details you make up.'

'Who'd want to be a cop?' They had to deal

with all sorts of problems from both sides of the case. Easier being a doctor, for sure.

'Some days I'd agree with you,' Megan replied wryly. 'Here's the ambulance. I'll let them see to you and we can catch up later. There're enough witnesses to help us go look for the man who did this.'

Ambulance. Hospital. Poking and prodding of her body. Not so wonderful. But she'd be given something for the pain in her head. That had to be a plus. Bring it on.

'You'll need my address.' She was going home tonight no matter what.

'Who did you say was in cubicle three?' Dr Lucas Tanner asked Chris, the nurse walking beside him in the emergency department. Surely it couldn't be Rosie. He hadn't seen her in ages. Not since his world had imploded three years ago and he'd left town to avoid everyone's sympathy.

'Rosie Carter. An emergency doctor on the choppers.'

Definitely one of his friends from way back when life was exciting and happy and filled with love, or so he'd believed.

'What's brought her here?'

'She was assaulted and robbed in a supermarket car park.'

'Are you serious?'

Of course he was. Lucas shivered. It was hideous just thinking about it, let alone imagining what Rosie must be feeling. One thing in her favour was that she was a toughie. Well, she used to be, anyway. But then he had no idea of what might've happened to her since they'd last seen each other. He knew from all that had gone on with him that life could throw horrible spears at people when they least expected them. Which was why he was a widower. A guilt-ridden one at that.

'Right, I've got this one.' Pulling back the curtain, he strode into the cubicle. 'Rosie, I can't believe it's you. Long time no see.'

She looked almost unrecognisable as the beautiful, funny woman he'd once known. Her face was pale and there was a large bruise covering her chin and another above her eyes. Her hands were shaking uncontrollably as her little fingers bent and straightened, bent and straightened. A tell that she was stressed he recognised from the past.

'Lucas?' Her eyes widened. 'It's really you?'

'Have I changed that much?' he quipped as he reached for the notes the paramedic had left on her bed. He probably had, given all the stress and pain he'd been through. But this was Rosie, part of the group of close friends he'd spent a year with, training in emergency medicine, and she knew some of what had gone down back then.

But not the reason for his guilt. No one knew that. Needing to put distance between them when his wonderful life had turned into a nightmare, he hadn't learned where she'd gone after he'd left Melbourne. He'd deliberately lost touch with everyone in the group except Brett, who'd refused to let him walk away completely. Now here was Rosie and he was pleased to see her, though not with the circumstances that had brought her into the department.

'Not really.'

That answer said more about her state of mind than just about anything could. No repartee today, something Rosie had always been good at. He'd sometimes wondered if that had been to keep people at a distance because she'd never been forthcoming about her private life. He hadn't a clue why that might've been and was probably so far off the mark it would be laughable if she knew his thoughts.

'Are you all right with me taking your case?' Technically, he didn't have to back off as they'd had nothing to do with each other for three years, but if Rosie had any issue with him checking her out then he was okay with it. 'I can get someone else, though you'll have to wait as everyone's tied up right now.'

He really should've looked her up when he'd returned home, along with the other two from the group he'd lost track of. He'd missed everyone and with his wife, May, gone, life got lonely at times. Very lonely, if he was being honest, but then he deserved to be. May would still be here if they hadn't got into that horrendous argument the night she'd died. Another reason to keep to himself—that way, he couldn't harm anyone he got close to.

'No problem at all.'

He hadn't realised he'd been holding his breath until Rosie said that. She had no issues with him. Not that he could think of a reason why she might. He had enough of his own to more than make up for anyone else's.

'Good.' Scanning the paramedic's notes, a relieved sigh escaped. 'You don't appear to have any major injuries, though I will order X-rays of your right hip and thigh to be certain. My biggest concern is concussion.' The notes didn't indicate a major skull trauma. There was a painful-looking area above her right eye where that massive bruise lay. He'd check that out. The bruise on her chin appeared minor. 'From the notes, it seems you took a fair whack on the head.' Her usually pretty face was marred by abrasions and, even more pronounced, shock.

'He hit me. Then I was thrown to the ground

when he sped away and my forehead took a slam against my car wheel. I hit the tarmac with my hip and thigh. But really, I'm all right. Just need to get home and go to bed.'

Slow down...take a breath, Rosie.

'No way. We're checking you over thoroughly and if I have the slightest concern about anything, including concussion, you're staying overnight.' Right now, he was her doctor, not her long ago friend, though as a pal he'd still insist on her staying in if necessary. Probably more so, because he found he didn't want anything going wrong for Rosie.

'Bossy britches.'

At least she wasn't arguing, which was more her style if he remembered correctly. And why wouldn't he? They'd been friends before May had died, before he'd withdrawn from the group of people that he'd been so keen to get to know on a deeper level. Especially this person, he remembered with shock. After four amazing years, cracks had started appearing in his marriage. Even so, he'd never overstepped the friendship line with Rosie. He'd still loved May, despite how they'd started going in different directions all of a sudden.

'You bet. Now, let me touch your skull and see what other damage there is.' As his fingers moved across her head, he spoke reassuringly.

'No soft spots, nor anything to suggest a bleed, but I want to be sure before accepting that as fact. We'll get this X-rayed too.'

Rosie's eyes flew open. 'Surely that's not necessary.'

'I'm erring on the side of caution.' Only doing his job. 'As I know you would, if our roles were reversed.' Her neck was tight. 'Move your head left. Right. Any pain when you do that?'

'No.' But she hadn't moved very far, and her fingers were doing their bend, straighten thing again.

He wasn't sure she was being totally honest with him. 'Any pain when I press here?' His fingers touched her neck by the right shoulder. The muscles were taut.

She shivered. 'No.' Then she sighed. 'It's tender but not painful.' So she wanted to pretend she was fine, but couldn't manage it. Hopefully, that meant the doctor side of her brain was coming to the fore.

'To be expected from impacting with anything solid and unforgiving.' Lucas shuddered at the thought of what that had been like. Sudden and hard, it would've been shocking to say the least. How could anybody do such harm to another person? To a complete stranger at that. It made his blood boil. There were some right losers out there. Nasty, even evil, people who thought they could do as they liked with no comeback. The problem being that many got away with it, which only encouraged others. As he felt Rosie's hip and thigh for possible fractures, he asked, 'Are the police onto your attacker?'

'The cop I talked to said they had plenty of witnesses to get started on looking for the car he was driving. Someone got the numberplate details. They were also going to check the supermarket's CCTV footage.'

Rosie didn't wince too much when he pressed on her hip and thigh. 'You've got massive bruising around this area, but nothing to suggest fractures.'

'Thanks.' A tear trickled out of the corner of her eye. Rosie slashed at it impatiently, only for another one to appear.

'Here.' Lucas felt his heart turn over as he handed across a box of tissues from the trolley. She'd know this was a normal reaction as the initial shock wore off, but this was Rosie and she'd hate for anyone to see her cry. Even him. She'd always been a tough cookie. But being assaulted would undermine anyone's strength for a while at least. 'Let it all out. I'll go organise the X-rays. Unless there's something else you need me to check?'

She tried to shake her head but her neck

wasn't having a bar of it, remaining rigid. 'No,' she whispered.

If only he could haul her into his arms and hug away her pain, but he was on duty. Plus, she might not like him to be so friendly after all this time. He'd never hugged her, although sometimes when things weren't going quite so well with May he'd wanted to wrap his arms around Rosie for a bit of comfort. Of course he'd resisted, not wanting anyone getting the wrong idea.

'I'm going to prescribe painkillers for you. Chris will bring them through.' While he worked on being sensible and ignoring this warmth he felt for Rosie.

'Those scrapes don't look deep so I doubt there'll be any scarring.' Chris began gently wiping the abrasions on Rosie's cheek to clean away the dirt and blood, something Lucas had an unusual urge to take over and do.

He really needed to get a life if this was how he reacted when catching up with a friend after so long out of contact. He looked around for something else to distract him and found nothing. Which was odd, since the group they'd both been a part of had got along well but there'd been nothing beyond friendship with any of them. It could be that after these past few years of carrying the guilt of letting May down that night, he was feeling relaxed with someone from that time who wouldn't want anything more from him than friendship. He could do that.

'Something to be grateful for, I suppose,' Rosie said to Chris.

The lassitude in her voice alarmed Lucas. He would do anything to take away her pain and shock. Going forward, how would she deal with the fact that a man had attacked her in broad daylight in a busy car park? It wasn't going to be easy over the coming weeks to accept what had happened without letting it interfere with her daily life. Where was the bastard who did this to her? He'd love ten minutes alone with him.

'I'll bring you some water to drink too,' Chris told Rosie.

She wiped her eyes. Her mouth was flat, her hands still shaky. 'Thanks. Can I have a triple vodka with that?'

Lucas didn't know if she was joking or serious; the despair in her voice was so gutting.

'I'll see what they've got at the pharmacy,' he told her around a tight smile. The last thing he felt like doing was smiling, but Rosie deserved better so he'd done his best. He couldn't have been very successful though because she barely looked at him. 'Back shortly.' He had Radiology to arrange and a prescription to organise.

It was hard to ignore how Rosie's sudden reappearance in his life had him standing up and taking more notice of her than he'd have expected, or had ever done before. He'd been totally devoted to May and the future they'd dreamed of: getting established in their careers, then having a home and family. Then May had got restless, started eyeing up the corporate ladder at the international company she worked for, and holes began appearing in their marriage. Problems he hadn't been prepared to admit to.

He'd been aware that Rosie was stunning, but so had all the men in their group. Today, seeing her in shock and as pale as his mother's white sheets, he'd felt a wrench over how lovely she truly was. Or was that his head playing games with him? Quite likely, as he wasn't usually into noticing women other than as patients, colleagues or friends. The pain over losing May had held him back from letting anyone get close again. That and the guilt. Especially the guilt. If only they hadn't had such a big argument. If only he'd remained calm and waited until they were together to talk about what she intended doing. He doubted it would've made any difference to her plans to move to Sydney, with or without him, but at least she'd still be alive.

When he returned to Rosie's cubicle, she was talking to a policewoman. 'Lucas, this is Megan.'

'Hello, Megan. I hope you catch the slimeball.'

'We're onto it.' Megan turned back to Rosie. 'Here are the keys to your car, which is still in the supermarket car park, all locked up.' She placed them on the table beside the bed. 'Is there someone who can collect it for you?'

Lucas waited for the answer. Was Rosie in a relationship? Was she married? The fact there was no ring on her finger meant nothing. She might not wear one while working. He'd heard she and her then partner, Cameron, had split about the time he'd left Melbourne.

'I could call one of my friends, but since my phone's gone I'm stuck. I don't know anyone's number off the top of my head.'

Sounded like she was on her own.

'Want me to collect the car? I'm knocking off any minute. I could take it home and bring it here tomorrow if you're staying overnight, which I think you should. You've got concussion and it wouldn't be wise to go home on your own.'

Was he making doubly sure she was single? No, he was simply being a responsible doctor, he growled to himself.

Rosie blinked. 'You don't have to do that. I'll pick it up tomorrow.' Then she gasped. 'I still haven't done anything about my bank cards.'

'I'll help you with that,' Lucas cut in. 'Whether you stay here or go home,' he added as she opened her mouth. 'It's what friends do.' They'd sort out what to do about the car later. It wasn't as important as cancelling the cards.

Megan beat Rosie to replying. 'Sounds like a good idea. After what you've been through, it would be nice to have someone giving you a hand with notifying the banks. If you're happy to give Lucas your details, that is?' Policewoman to the fore.

'No problem whatsoever. We're old friends.' Rosie's mouth tipped up into a small, sincere smile.

His heart lightened. He'd be useful to her in a capacity other than the medical one. 'Right, that's it. I'm officially done for the day, so let's start getting everything sorted while you wait to be taken to Radiology.'

'I'll leave you to it.' Megan handed Rosie a card. 'Here's my contact number. Let me know when you go home because we need to get a full statement from you and it takes a couple of hours at least.'

Rosie's eyes widened at that. Then she sagged into her pillow. 'Thank you for your support. The whole thing's been a bit of an eye-opener.'

'I'm sure it has. I'll get out of the way now. Take care and we'll talk tomorrow.'

As Megan headed out, Lucas glanced at Rosie and saw her shiver. 'Hey, you're doing well. If there's anything good to come out of this, it's that we've caught up again.'

'I've often wondered where you'd got to and what you were doing. I miss everyone from our trainee group. We had some great times together, including everyone's partners.'

'A lot of study and a few too many parties,' he replied with a laugh.

Until his wife had died, and then nothing was ever the same for any of them. Everyone had missed her, and went out of their way to support him, but his grief and guilt had been too much for him to bear all the sympathy, so he'd left for Sydney, and then gone out of the country a year later. Sadness welled up. Another of his and May's difficulties had been that she'd thought he spent more time with the group than with her. He couldn't argue with that totally, but she'd spent plenty of evenings with her work colleagues too.

'We had to let go of the tension brought on by dealing with dreadful cases at work somehow. Though I don't seem to need to do that these days. Must be used to the horrors of the job now.' She stared at him for a moment. 'How long have you been working here?'

'I returned from the States two months ago and came on board here three weeks later.'

'You enjoyed working over there?'

'I did, but my contract was up so I figured it was time to come home and make some decisions about my house.' Time to finally face the past, and hopefully move on. He'd hidden away too long and had missed out on a lot with his family. 'The last tenants didn't exactly take care of the place so I'm fixing up the damage and painting the place throughout.' It had turned out to be harder than he'd expected, being back in the house where there were so many memories of May to haunt him.

'How's that working out?'

He hated the sympathy in her eyes. 'Great,' he lied. 'Even if I say so myself, I'm not too bad at replacing dented plasterboards. My brother, Leon, gives me a hand when he's not at work.'

'Go you.' Rosie yawned. 'I want to go home.'

She sounded petulant, nothing like the woman he remembered, but then she hadn't been attacked back then either.

'How's your vision?'

She blinked at him. 'Mostly fine, though every now and then it's a little blurry.'

That sealed it. 'You're staying overnight.'

She sighed in resignation. 'I'd better let Steve know I won't be at work tomorrow.'

'Your boss?' he asked, since there hadn't been any mention of an important other person so far.

'Head of Victoria Rescue. He's available for staff twenty-four-seven.'

That must be a pain in the backside for the man.

'I've met him a couple of times when he's come in here with a patient. He's a good guy. Do you know his number?'

Her face lit up for the first time. 'It's about the only one I do.'

'Want me to call him?'

'Would you? Right now, I just want to curl up and go to sleep, but what if images of that ugly wide-eyed face fill my head while I'm out?'

Lucas felt his heart tighten. She was more shaken than she'd let on and it seemed to be catching up with her. He was surprised it had taken so long. He squeezed her shoulder lightly as a pal, not the doctor he'd been earlier.

'I reckon you'll fall into such a deep sleep nothing will affect you.' Hopefully, that would be the case. But this was only the first night after what had happened. There'd be plenty ahead when her fears might be realised. 'But first I'll grab a wheelchair and take you to Radiology, where we can sit in a corner while we wait for your X-rays to be done and make some calls to the banks after I've talked to Steve.'

'You've got everything covered.'

Why wouldn't he? He wasn't the one this had happened to.

'I hope so.'

'Let's do it.' Rosie sat up and swung her legs over the side of the bed. At least she tried to swing them, but the look on her face said it hurt to move.

'Take it slowly,' Lucas warned. 'We don't know for sure there's not a serious injury in your hip.' Though he doubted it. He'd seen enough fractured hips and thighs to know, but he wanted to be absolutely sure. She did not need any more pain than she was already dealing with. That was the friend side of his brain, not the medical one, which was odd considering he was a doctor first and foremost in ED.

You've signed off for the day.

True. He'd stick with Rosie while she had the X-rays and then was moved to the general ward. Because that *was* happening. Unless she would agree to go home with him.

Where did that idea come from?

Friend side of his brain, remember? It would be a lot wiser to stick to the medical side for now. Who knew if Rosie gave a fig about friends from the past?

Rosie rolled over and groaned. 'Wrong way, idiot.' The bruises on her hip had a lot to say for themselves. Thankfully, nothing else was wrong with her hip.

On the other side of the bed, Lucas chuckled. 'Want a warning sign drawn up?'

She remembered that chuckle—deep, with the ability to drag people into his aura. Everyone had liked Lucas. He just had a way of making a person feel special for the time he was with them. Even her, and she was a sceptic when it came to believing men would treat her well without turning out to be wrong about them. He'd been married to May and there was nothing behind his manner except camaraderie. May had come first and everyone knew it. Sometimes she been a little jealous of them as a couple; she'd known she and Cameron weren't as good together because she was afraid to let him that close.

What happened to May had been horrific and watching Lucas fall apart piece by piece afterwards was hard for everyone. Had he managed to move on? Reached a point where he could get through the day without reliving his time with May? She hoped so for his sake.

Carefully rolling the other way, she dug deep for a grin, because that was what she did with friends, put on a determinedly happy face to dodge the unpleasant questions they might want to ask. 'Can you make it a verbal one so if I'm asleep I'll still know to avoid my right side?'

'Onto it.' His smile faded. 'How are you feeling, really?'

She thought about it. 'Tired. Still angry. But more than anything, I'm feeling bewildered.'

Lucas straightened in his chair. 'Why?'

'To think there I was, about to unload my trolley of groceries and go home, when instead my world was tipped upside down within moments by a selfish idiot with nothing better to do than attack and rob me.'

Lucas took her hand and enclosed it in both his. It was a caring gesture that surprised her, but then she was out of kilter at the moment so could explain away the sense of belonging his touch gave her. She liked that more than she'd have believed.

'It's not something anyone expects or can imagine until it happens. You'll get through this, Rosie. You never did take nonsense from anyone, and I know this'll be the same.'

His hands were so warm and soft. It was kind of nice having him hold her when she felt so out of sorts. Good pals were the best, and hard to come by. Especially for her as she was cautious about getting close to people and then being let down. If her father could do that to her after her mother died, then anyone could, and enough had.

'You just need to get through the coming days

and you'll be back to yourself. Don't be impatient, Rosie.'

He made it sound so easy. Her eyes filled. Another sign she wasn't her usual self.

'You do remember me well.' Patience had never been one of her better qualities.

'My memory's not so bad. It hasn't been that long since we were working long hours, night and day, in the ED and giving each other hell about getting everything right. Along with the others, I've missed you and those times. We were damned serious about our work and qualifying, and always there for each other. Even our partners were part of that.'

A shadow crossed his face. Thinking about May? Or his life before he'd lost his wife in a shocking road accident? Her heart went out to him. It had been an awful time.

To fill the sudden silence, she continued. 'In the department *and* out of it.'

Yes, those were the days when it was all work and not a lot of play, but when they had played the five of them had always had a blast. Along with their partners on the occasions they'd joined in the fun. Rosie hadn't got to know May all that well. She'd been working for a large law firm and the only subject she'd ever talked about in a relaxed manner was her job. She'd always come across as perfect in all she did, both personally and professionally, sometimes making Rosie feel inadequate—not in terms of her career, but in her relationship with Cameron. She wasn't perfect in the slightest.

Cameron was a great guy, specialising in cardiology. She'd really liked him but worried he'd find her lacking in what he wanted in a life partner, so when she'd left Melbourne to work for a year in Perth to gain more experience she'd gone without him and that was the end of them. She'd hurt him big time and still felt bad about that. She'd cared a lot for him, but not enough to take that final step to for ever. There hadn't been anyone since. She couldn't seem to find it in her to find 'the one' who she could trust to settle down with, to love for ever and maybe have a family with.

After the remote way her father had raised her and her brother, Johnno, after their mother died, she didn't have it in her to trust anyone totally with her heart. If her dad could withdraw from her then anyone could, and she wasn't exposing herself to that degree of pain again. She'd only been eight, and Johnno fourteen, at the time. It had been as though their dad had died too, for all the love he'd shown them after the day of their mother's funeral. Virtually none, other than providing food on the table and money for anything they'd needed. She'd grieved for two parents from that day on. At least she and Johnno had always been close.

'I think being able to decompress together was what got us all through the difficult shifts.' Lucas laid her hand on the bed and leaned back in the chair, drawing her attention back to him and away from the past that haunted her to this day. 'Because there were certainly moments when each of us wanted to walk away and find a *normal* job.'

He was referring to those times when one of them lost a patient, despite doing everything possible, and more, to prevent that outcome. Yes, every medical doctor faced those. Lucas had faced a different pain too. Losing May had devastated him.

So had he found a new partner yet? Or was he still struggling to cope with what he'd lost? She didn't feel she had the right to ask. They had been good pals, but chances were they wouldn't be as close as they'd once been. Too much time had gone by for that. But it was so good to see him. She hadn't realised how much she had missed him. And the rest of the group. They'd had some wonderful times, unwinding over a drink, laughing and talking like there was no tomorrow. But they'd all struggled with May's death. Losing one of their own had been a huge shock.

CHAPTER TWO

LUCAS STARED OUT of the window onto the street beyond his fence as the microwave dealt with his eggs. 'Unreal' was the word that came to mind when he thought about his last patient of the day. Day? It was well after nine and he'd been home barely thirty minutes. All because he'd caught up with an old friend in unusual circumstances. Unusual in that he didn't often come across anyone he knew when working in the ED. The hospital was one of many in Melbourne, and not all his friends had gone into emergency medicine. Only those he'd known here back when they were qualifying.

His blood boiled when he thought about what that cretin had done to Rosie. He'd often dealt with victims of random crime through work, but this had happened to someone he knew and that made it more horrific. Rosie was a special friend he'd got on well with until the group had gone their separate ways to further their careers, and he'd gone away to cope with losing May.

He'd feel the same if it had been any of the others coming into the ED after a similar experience. Wouldn't he? Why the doubt? Rosie hadn't meant anything more to him back then, had she? He'd been very happy married to May and hadn't looked at any other woman, hadn't wanted to. Though he had noticed Rosie's stunning looks and enjoyed talking to her about anything and everything too.

Despite the increasing arguments between them, he'd still loved May. When they married, they'd agreed to stay in Melbourne until he'd established his career in emergency medicine and so they'd bought the house. Then she'd decided there was only one way her career in law was going and that was to the top of the international company she worked for. Not that she'd discussed it with him, and when she'd told him over the phone that fatal night that she was leaving for Sydney within a fortnight and he could follow when he'd sorted his job out he'd been hurt and lashed out with angry words. That and the fact he was going to be late home to celebrate her promotion were why she'd said to hell with him, she was going to celebrate with people who mattered and hung up on him.

Beep, beep, beep.

Dinner is cooked.

Not quite. He gave the eggs a light stir with

the whisk and stuck the bowl back in the microwave for thirty seconds. After buttering the toast, he took a mouthful of beer from his bottle and returned to staring outside.

Once in the ward, Rosie had fought falling asleep, but in the end the shock she'd had and the medications she'd taken had won out and she'd nodded off.

He'd stayed for another half hour in case she woke and wanted to talk about what had happened, but she'd been out for the count. It was good she'd succumbed to staying in overnight without much of an argument. It wouldn't have been wise for her to be home alone tonight. He would've offered her a bed here if that had been the case, but doubted she'd have taken him up on it. Always an independent woman, Rosie used to hate being beholden to anyone, which he'd never understood. After a particularly bad day in the ED she'd always tried to hide her emotions, but he and the others got to recognise her tell. Her little fingers would bend and straighten numerous times, as had been the case tonight.

Beep, beep, beep.

'Shut up.' His appetite was disappearing. Not that scrambled eggs were a real dinner, but he often cheated after a long day in the department. It seemed so pointless going to the hassle of preparing vegetables and steak or a casserole just for himself. Far easier to heat something already prepared from the supermarket. By the time he'd left Rosie earlier tonight he couldn't get enthused about going into the store to choose dinner from a freezer either.

His phone announced the arrival of a text. Rosie? He'd left her his number in case she wanted anything, but as she didn't have her phone she was limited on what she could do, though two of the nurses had been quick to say she could use theirs.

Not Rosie. It was Leon, his brother. He wasn't disappointed. He *wasn't*. He was not looking for another woman to come into his life. His heart wasn't strong enough to fall in love again, nor to believe everything would work out all right. If it could go bad with May then it would with any other woman he came to care about.

'Hey, dude, how's it going?'

'Not bad. The roof went on at number twenty-three today, so we can get cracking there.' Leon owned a small building company that was always in high demand. 'I've got half the guys working on the finishing touches for the other house. I've got to go over plans for the next place too. The customers want things done in the kitchen that are going to be tricky, to say the least.'

'There's always something, isn't there?'

'Makes the job interesting. How was your day?'

'Same old, same old.' Apart from Rosie turning up in his life again. But that didn't change a thing. Hopefully, they'd get to catch up a bit but he couldn't see them spending much time together. They had gone in different directions three years ago and he was looking at her as though everything had remained the same. But it wouldn't have. It hadn't for him. The time spent in San Fran had been busy with work and getting out and about in the towns further inland. He'd taken up cycling, which had led to some hair-raising rides around the city and beyond. 'I caught up with one of my friends from training days, which was cool.'

'Good. Someone else to keep you here. Are you heading out this way tomorrow?'

He had intended to, but now he hesitated. 'Not sure.' Rosie might need her car once she was back on her feet. Plus, he couldn't deny the inexplicable need grabbing at him to make sure she was recovering well and wasn't too stressed over what had happened. Strange how he felt a little lighter in the heart tonight. 'If I do, it'll be later in the day.' Unless Rosie wanted him to hang around. But then why would she ask that of him? Surely she had other friends to be there for her? He did like to make sure things were okay though. It was his doctor brain coming to the fore, not his friend side. He shrugged. Really? No idea.

'How are you feeling this morning?' Lucas asked Rosie the next morning when she took the ward phone the nurse held out to her.

Even though he couldn't see her, Rosie shrugged dramatically. 'A bit sore but otherwise all good.' The painkillers had worked a treat. Her mind was a mess about the assault and how suddenly her day had been tossed about, but that wasn't going to be sorted any time soon. Not that she intended letting her assailant screw with her wellbeing, but she understood that it mightn't be as easy as she'd like to forget what he'd done. 'I'm heading home shortly.' She couldn't wait to get out of here. It was one thing to be a doctor and look out for her patients, but quite different being on the receiving end of all the attention.

'I'll come by and pick you up.'

Hello? When did Lucas get to tell her what she was doing?

'No need. I'll grab a cab.'

'Found your wallet, have they?' he retorted.

'No, but I do have cash in my glovebox.' She'd take the taxi to the supermarket car park and collect the car. 'And before you ask, I can get into my apartment too.' The swipe card was on the same keyring as her car key. Last night she'd somehow managed to convince Lucas he didn't have to pick up her vehicle, though she wasn't sure how she'd managed that as he'd been quite persistent at first.

'Rosie, how about I give you a lift to your car this morning? It's not out of my way and I'd like to see how you're doing.' He sounded tired, as though he hadn't slept much last night.

She relented. She told herself it was because it had been good to catch up with Lucas again, and yes, she'd like to spend more time finding out what he'd been up to in the intervening years since they'd seen one another. Returning to Melbourne at the end of her twelve-month contract in Perth had been the right thing to do. She'd missed her brother as well as her two girlfriends and their families. She didn't want to be anywhere else. Melbourne was home. Something she'd needed when she couldn't risk falling in love.

Wanting to catch up some more with Lucas had nothing to do with the fact she'd thought about him every time she'd woken during the night. Visualising his endearing smile every time she'd started to think about why she was in hospital and not curled up in her own bed had calmed her instantly. It felt good to have a friend, albeit one from a while ago, by her side at the moment. Her two girlfriends were unaware of what had happened as she hadn't been able to phone them, something she'd rectify with her laptop when she got home.

'I'll be ready and waiting when you come by.'

'That wasn't so hard, was it? Are you free to go shortly?'

'Yes, I've had the all-clear. I'll meet you outside the main entrance.' She had no idea how long it would take him to get here. 'Where do you live?'

'A few blocks away in Parkville.'

'You're kidding? My apartment's in Parkville too.' The hospital was also in Parkville. Lucas would be here shortly. 'I'll make my way downstairs when I hang up.'

'Give me thirty, will you? I'm out walking the neighbour's dog. We're not far from home so I won't be too long. Unless Molly misbehaves, that is.' Lucas laughed, that deep vibrant sound that had her skin heating when it had no reason to. Or did it? She'd always found him attractive and sexy but had ignored that because they were both in other relationships.

Reacting to him after all this time was weird. Perhaps she could put it down to the bang on the head she'd received yesterday.

'See you soon.' She hung up before she could

get into a deeper mire of heat and out-of-line thinking.

Handing the phone back to the nurse, she said, 'Thanks for that. I'm going to have to do some shopping ASAP. It's weird not having a phone.'

'I lost mine for a couple of days once and thought my world had stopped. There's so much day-to-day info on it that I was lost without it,' the nurse told her.

That was the scary thing, Rosie conceded as she headed to the lift to go downstairs and wait for Lucas. There was a load of information on her phone that she needed; she was going to struggle till she had another phone and got everyone's numbers sorted. Starting with Lucas's. She wasn't losing touch with him again. Good friends were important and due to her lack of trust she didn't have many.

Johnno kept insisting she only had to get together with his best mate and she wouldn't need anyone else, but no way was she going down that path. One date with Will Clark had been one too many. He was arrogant beyond belief, and still called occasionally to remind her of what she was missing out on by not dating him. Now her brother was getting married in a couple of weeks' time, the pressure was on to partner Will to the wedding. She reckoned it was because he couldn't find anyone else who'd go with him, but he'd never admit that. Johnno really wanted her to be as happy as he was and said she'd be seated next to Will at the reception unless she brought someone else. So far, she hadn't found anyone to ask, being a bit embarrassed that she even had to do so.

Lucas.

His name slammed into her aching head. He would make an ideal partner for the wedding. Would he, though? They wouldn't come across as being in a close relationship and, bossy britches that he was, her brother wouldn't accept anything less.

Sometimes he took the older loving brother role too far. Mostly she was happy with him looking out for her and returned it in kind because they'd both lost so much when their mother passed. Turning to their father whenever they'd needed a hug and instead getting a blank stare had undermined their security and their belief that they were automatically loved without restraint by those who should have known better. At least they'd had each other to stumble through life with, until Johnno left home to go to university. Then she'd been on her own and very lonely until it was her turn to leave. She'd often wondered if her father had even noticed she'd gone.

Back to Lucas. It was too soon to be thinking of asking him to help her out of her predicament with the wedding. They'd caught up only last night. He'd regret wanting to help her out today if she put a proposition to him about accompanying her and would probably make sure he was always busy from now on so he didn't have a spare moment to play catchup. That was the last thing she wanted. It was the first time someone from her past had come back into her life and looked happy about being there. Early days, but a girl could dream of more. She knew of people who had friends they rarely caught up with but when they did it was as though they'd never been apart.

After her few relationships she'd come to the conclusion that friendships were far safer. Longer lasting and easy to come and go with. Whereas the two serious relationships she'd had had been fun and exciting before they'd slowly become awkward because she was afraid to commit and thereby expose herself to more hurt. She'd let down the men she'd partnered up with, but hadn't been able to find it within her to open up and fall in love. It was far too risky.

'Hey, there.' Lucas was striding towards her looking so handsome in denim shorts and a green shirt that her hands tightened at her sides. Those long, suntanned legs of his were seriously sexy!

She would not think about Lucas like this. Not

so soon after meeting up again. Not ever, really. He was a friend. If she did get a little closer than was wise, then she'd only lose a friend when she pulled the plug, as she always did with relationships. Okay, how about a handsome friend?

Rosie couldn't help it. She laughed.

'Glad to hear that sound. You must be feeling better than when I left to go home last night.' He gave her a quick hug.

Too quick for her liking, but he was being the sensible one at the moment. She'd get there soon.

'I've lost the dizzy head and the pain is under control.'

'Get much sleep?'

'On and off. I didn't realise how noisy hospital wards could be at night.' There'd been a young woman in the bed next to hers who'd kept pressing the bell for help with one problem or another.

'Says you, who's spent many hours in them over the years.'

'I don't think I ever thought about how noisy it got, to be honest. Something to remember if I return to hospital work.' She walked beside him to a taxi parked on the other side of the road. 'I thought you were picking me up in your vehicle.'

'This way I can drive you home in your car and then walk back to my house. It's only a few streets from your apartment.' Lucas held the door open for her.

He was being very considerate, but she wasn't incapable of looking out for herself.

'I'm good to drive. I can drop you off at your place on the way.'

'Okay.' Lucas headed around to the other side of the cab, looking unmoved by her snappy reply.

She should be grateful he hadn't made a big deal out of it. As he joined her in the back of the taxi she looked away, already regretting being short with him and embarrassed by how much she enjoyed the view of his tall, lean body and thick curly hair falling over his brow. As for the light stubble on his chin? Her fingers tightened to keep the urge to touch it under control.

'Anything you might need before we pick up your car?' he asked as the driver pulled away from the kerb.

'I need a phone sooner rather than later. I'll have to talk to the insurance company, but I can't wait until they go through the process of paying out.' Another thought crossed her mind. 'I have no idea what's happened to my groceries either. They were in the shopping trolley when I was attacked.' What with all that had gone down, they'd completely slipped her mind. 'Hopefully, someone put the bags in my car before it was locked.'

'We'll find out soon enough,' Lucas said. 'If

you do need to do another shop I'll lend you my card. Same goes for the phone.'

Rosie shook her head and instantly regretted it as pain shot through her neck. 'I don't seem to be getting my head around the consequences of what happened. I'd totally forgotten I have no access to money until I go into the bank on Monday and withdraw some. As I mentioned last night, there's a bit of cash in the car.' Nowhere near enough to buy a phone, more like a loaf of bread and something for dinner.

'How about I get a couple hundred bucks out and you can repay me when everything's back to normal? If you want to replace your phone today, I'll use my card.'

Her heart melted for this generous man. 'Thank you. I'll take you up on the offer of cash, just in case something happens and I need money urgently.'

'It's no big deal, Rosie.' He cleared his throat. 'It's what any decent friend would do.' He sounded as though he was trying to convince himself of where their relationship stood. Which made no sense whatsoever.

She might've gone off on a tangent regarding how she felt about Lucas, but she'd taken a hell of a bang on the head yesterday so anything was possible.

'You're right.' She leaned back and closed her

eyes, hoping to clear her mind of anything but getting home and unwinding from the tension tugging at her from all directions. Thankfully, no image of those frightening, wide staring eyes belonging to her assailant filled her mind, as it had done during the night whenever she'd managed to get comfortable and start to doze off.

The man was ugly—and terrifying. His eyes had appeared as big as saucers. His mouth had been contorted into an evil smile. She shivered and opened her eyes to stare beyond the taxi window. It had been far nicer waking to the image of Lucas's face in her mind.

Ha, that was why she was coming up with weird and wonderful thoughts about Lucas. He'd been shoving the other man away from her thoughts.

'Think you should get some fresh milk,' Lucas noted as they checked Rosie's groceries that someone had placed in the back of her car at some point. Probably one of the cops had seen to everything. He reached for a pack of ham lying in one of the bags. 'This mightn't be too great either. It's not exactly cool in here.'

'I'll toss it when I get back to my apartment. I've still got some milk so I won't bother going into the supermarket now.' She closed the boot and headed for the driver's side. 'I just want to get home.'

That was the closest she'd come to admitting she was still out of sorts, Lucas noted. Definitely fading.

'And I'll walk from there.' He got in on the passenger's side and belted up before going for a neutral topic. 'How long have you been in your apartment?'

'Nearly two years. I bought it when I returned from Perth. It was a no-brainer as Melbourne's home for me and my brother and my closest friends are here.'

'What about your parents? Where are they?' He knew next to nothing about her private life. It hadn't been what most of the group talked about, which was usually work and the people there.

Rosie glanced at him, then turned back to stare out of the windscreen. 'Mum died when I was eight.'

'That must've been hard.' To lose a parent so young was beyond comprehension. How did a wee girl grow up and deal with life without a mother at her side? 'You still have your father?'

'He died five years ago.' She started the car and backed out of the parking bay, then drove carefully through the busy car park and out onto the road.

He didn't push for more information about her

parents. It was obviously a touchy subject, and he knew only too well how it felt when people started asking questions about things he didn't want to answer—usually to do with May and his life since her passing. Even harder to take was the sympathy over his loss as it ramped up his guilt and had him wanting to hide away until everyone left him alone.

'Is your brother older or younger?'

'Six years older. He was the rebellious one. Not so much these days though.'

'Which makes you the good one.'

'Yep. Too much sometimes, I think, but it's what got me through everything until I left home to go to university. And ever since,' she added quietly.

Too quietly, but he thought he'd heard correctly. He definitely got the sadness behind what she'd said. He wasn't asking for more information and having her shut down completely. This was a side to Rosie he'd not known before. Though there were times she'd been uptight, which he'd put down to issues at work, otherwise her behaviour and attitude had always been cool and calm. Not your party all night type, despite always being there when they'd all got together to let their hair down. Nor had she been outspoken or difficult when it came to awkward situations on the job. Rosie mostly got on with what had to be done and had a lot of quiet fun when they were off work and unwinding.

'Are you saying you weren't good once you left home?' He grinned to show he wasn't being serious.

She shrugged, then grimaced. The shoulder that had taken the impact yesterday must still hurt like crazy. 'I doubt I know how to be really badly behaved, which makes me sound boring.'

Faking a yawn, he said, 'If you say so.'

Rosie was definitely not boring. Not if the way he'd spent hours thinking about her since first walking into the cubicle and seeing her in the ED yesterday was an indicator. Either that or boring was his go-to woman. Something he knew was not true. Exciting and sexy were more his style. Except this was Rosie, a friend, not a woman to start a hot fling with. Except she was so damned sexy. And stunning even when battered and bruised, once he'd got over the shock of seeing her again. How was it she was still single?

Rosie tossed him a tight smile. 'Thanks, pal.'

'Just saying.' He grinned, working on quietening the heat building in his blood. 'What do you think you'll do for the rest of the day?'

'I'll get on the laptop and email various people about what's happened. Other than that, not a lot. Unless—' She stopped.

Lucas waited, and when it became apparent Rosie wasn't going to finish that sentence he said, 'Are you worried about how this has affected you emotionally?' Her mind had to be in overdrive, going over what had happened and how suddenly her world had been flipped. The attack had come out of the blue and would surely have her looking over her shoulder whenever she was out amongst strangers for quite a while.

'A little bit.'

'If you want to talk about it, I'm available any time.' Which meant he wouldn't go around to Leon's later if she took him up on the offer, but that wasn't a problem. Leon would understand.

'I'll be fine.' She indicated right and turned into a parking area beneath a small apartment block. 'I *am* fine.'

He doubted it, but there was nothing he could do if she didn't want to talk to him.

'I'll leave you my number anyway, in case there's anything you might need.'

'My friends will be here once they learn what's happened. So will Johnno, though I'm not sure I want to see him today.'

'Why not?'

As she parked in a space she muttered, 'He'll have plenty to say about a couple of things.'

'Are you talking about the attack?' Her brother

would have to be an ass if he was going to criticise her for what had happened.

'What? Oh, no, not that. Just a family matter.' She winced as she got out of the car.

A scream rent the air.

Lucas spun around and headed for the entrance. 'What's that about?'

Rosie was right beside him. 'Someone's on the ground on the other side of the road. Looks like a young woman.' She was charging over the road, her own pain apparently forgotten.

Lucas was right beside her. 'What happened?' he asked a teenage boy as they reached the woman sprawled on the footpath, groaning and writhing in pain.

'He hit my mummy with his skateboard,' a young girl said.

'I didn't mean to,' the teenager muttered. 'I came off my board and it flew at her.'

Lucas dropped to his knees beside the woman, Rosie doing the same on the other side. 'Hello, I'm Lucas, a doctor, and this is Rosie, also a doctor.'

'My leg. The pain's excruciating,' groaned the woman as she tried to reach for her knee.

Rosie covered her hand, pulled it away gently. 'Easy. You could cause more damage by moving your leg. And more pain.' She glanced at Lucas. 'You're the one with a phone.'

He pulled it from his pocket as he studied the lower leg before him. The shin appeared to be shattered, pieces of bone poking through the skin. 'The skateboard must've hit hard.' Damned hard. The angle would have had a huge impact.

Rosie nodded in agreement. Blood oozed from lacerations where the bone had come through. Her fingers were carefully checking the shin and then the knee. 'What's your name?' she asked the woman.

'Mummy's called Freya,' the little girl said before her mother could get a word in. 'Is she going to be all right?' For someone so young she didn't appear too distressed by the sight of blood or the sound of her mother's groans, though she might come down to earth with a thud any moment.

'Mummy will need to see a doctor. Do you live near here?' Someone would need to come and get the girl.

'We were going to see Grandma when he hit her with his board.'

'I didn't hit her!' shouted the teenager.

'Hey, come and talk to me,' a passerby said to the lad and led him a little further along the footpath and away from the girl.

As he filled in the emergency services on what had happened Lucas noted a small crowd had now gathered around. 'Freya needs an ambulance ASAP,' he told the man on the other end of the phone, then shoved his phone in his pocket. 'Any pain anywhere else?' he asked Freya.

'Can't really tell with the leg. Think I landed on my left arm and shoulder when I went down. Everything's hurting.'

Rosie laid a hand on her right arm. 'You're doing so well. Once the ambulance is here they'll give you oxygen to make your breathing easier, and painkillers to help too.'

Lucas glanced at Rosie and felt a surge of admiration at her calmness, despite her own painful injuries. Something warm slid through him. No doubt about it, she was special. Mentally shaking his head at the senseless heat filling him, he moved Freya's arm, then checked the shoulder for any sign of tension. 'Shoulder's good,' he told the young woman. 'Though there are some bruises appearing.'

'Better than more broken bones,' Rosie said.

'What happened to you?' the little girl asked Rosie, eyeing her bruised face.

'Anna, don't be nosy,' Freya said, her words drawn out around the pain filling her, as though good parenting was more important than what had happened to her. Which it probably was, thought Lucas.

Rosie drew a breath and gave the girl a smile. 'I fell over and hit my head.'

'Weren't you looking where you were going?' Anna's eyes were filled with interest.

Rosie's laugh was tight. 'Something like that.'

A siren filled the air and diverted Anna from further questions.

'Freya, is there someone I can call to come and get Anna?' Lucas asked.

'Mum.' She groaned out the number for him to tap into his phone and within moments it was all sorted.

'Your mother's on her way,' he told the stressed Freya.

'Thank you.'

Lucas recognised the two paramedics leaping out of the ambulance to hurry towards them. 'Hey, Lucas, Rosie. Someone got lucky having both of you here,' said Taylor as she knelt down beside Freya. 'Fill me in.'

Lucas looked to Rosie and gave her a nod to go ahead. She was a rescue doctor and knew what was required now the paras were here.

'This is Freya,' Rosie told Taylor. 'A skateboard slammed into her shin and there are multiple fractures in a very small area.'

'Any other injuries?'

'Not that Lucas or I could find, though Freya says she hurts all over.'

'From what she's told us, she hit the ground hard,' Lucas added.

The second paramedic, Jordan, was placing a mask attached to an oxygen tank over Freya's face. 'Freya, we'll get your breathing sorted and then administer something for the pain, okay?'

Freya nodded once, then grimaced and tried to pull the mask away.

Lucas lifted it a little way from her mouth. 'Easy. Are you trying to tell us something?'

'Don't like mask.'

'Give it a minute and you'll feel a little better.' He slipped it back in place and stood up. 'We'll get out of the way and let you two get on with the job.'

Rosie was talking to Taylor. 'Do you need a hand wrapping that leg in plastic before we go?' It would keep the bone pieces from moving too much when Freya was shifted onto the trolley.

'Or help to get her on board the ambulance?' Lucas asked.

Taylor shook her head. 'Jordan and I will manage, thanks. We heard what happened to you last night, Rosie. It's appalling. Are you coping all right?'

'I'm getting there. Lucas has been great helping me with a couple of things.'

Taylor hadn't finished. 'You take care, okay? See you when you're back at work.'

Rosie straightened and rubbed her thigh. 'Monday.'

Not if that hip was still giving her trouble, Lucas thought grimly, then realised he had no say in the matter and Rosie would no doubt go to work, sore hip or not.

'Grandma!' shrieked Anna. 'Mummy's hurt.'

A worried-looking woman stumbled as Anna threw herself at her. 'Settle, sweetheart. Where's Mummy?'

Lucas and Rosie approached her at the same time. 'I'm Lucas, and this is Rosie. We're both doctors and saw to Freya until the ambulance arrived. They'll be taking her to the Parkville hospital shortly.'

'Her leg's hurt, Grandma.' Anna was clinging to the older woman's hand.

She asked, 'How bad is it?'

'She's probably going to need surgery, I'm afraid. The lower bones in one leg are broken.' That was as much as he was telling her. It was up to the orthopaedic surgeon to fill in the gaps once they knew the full extent of the injuries.

'Come on, Grandma. You've got to see Mummy.'

'Thank you for helping Freya,' the woman said as she was tugged away by her granddaughter.

'Let's go. There's nothing more we can do here.' Lucas took Rosie's hand and led her through the onlookers and across the road before realising what he was doing and dropped her hand fast. 'I'll carry your groceries up to your apartment before I head away.'

'I'll let you do that. Plus make coffee if you're interested.' This time Rosie gave him one of her soft smiles that sneaked in under his radar without any effort.

He liked it, but wasn't sure he should. It could get him into all sorts of trouble if he wasn't careful. But then *careful* was his middle name these days. Still, he wasn't risking anything by having a coffee with Rosie, surely?

'I rarely say no to a decent coffee.' Though this was one time he probably should but didn't want to. Presuming she made good coffee, it was the best pick-me-up he knew, other than a glass of cool wine after a long day at work. But that was for another time. This was morning and he had jobs to do when he got home. 'Make it black.'

'Pop those bags on the bench,' Rosie said when they entered her apartment.

The place had him drawing a breath.

'This is stunning.' Like its owner. The front of the unit was basically all glass, allowing light to flow in, and there wasn't a dark corner to be seen. A deck ran the length of the front wall and the worn furniture out there suggested it was well used. After placing the grocery bags on the bench, he stepped outside and gazed at the view. 'Not bad.'

'I fell for it the moment I walked in through the main door.' Rosie stood beside him. 'I had to have it, and when the agent told me there was another offer going in that day I kind of panicked and paid over the top for it, but I've never regretted it.'

So she could lose control over her feelings? Interesting. He hadn't seen that side to her.

'No lawns to worry about mowing. Though nowhere to grow your vegetables either.'

'That's what fruit and veg shops are for.' She left him standing there and went to turn on the coffee machine, looking more at ease than he'd seen since catching up with her last night. Home was obviously her go-to place. She'd said she needed to get back here but he hadn't realised quite how much she'd meant it. The décor suggested a lot of input from her, modern and refined yet comfortable and cosy, with warm pink and soft green shades. There were two paintings of outback Australia with the red dirt and sparse trees standing out brightly.

The emotion they brought about had him holding his breath. 'Who painted these?'

'Dad.'

He turned to study Rosie. She was tense and her face devoid of emotion. Okay, he knew when to back off, but there was a lot he'd like to find out one day if she ever relaxed enough to tell him.

Looking around the room, he realised there were no photos. Odd, to say the least. Who didn't have some photos of family or friends to be seen by everyone? He knew she'd never shared much about herself with any of them back when he'd known her before, but this didn't add up when the apartment drew him in with its warmth and cosiness. Something wasn't right, or was he getting confused over this new awareness of Rosie? He wondered what her bedroom was like. There might be photos in there, just for her to enjoy. He wasn't even thinking about a bed. No, he wasn't.

The apartment was nothing like the house he was currently doing up—large, functional and relaxing in a simple way. The relaxing came about only when he had time to do nothing, which wasn't often. The plans he and May had had for altering the lounge, dining area and kitchen into a family space had taken a back seat. Now he was focused on making the place comfortable and modern, and easy to sell to a growing family. Though the longer he was here the more he wondered if he might stay permanently because it was great being back amongst his family and friends, who were still living all over the city. Selling might be off the cards.

Except for the memories. Those still haunted him on bad days. Last week, when he'd knocked down an internal wall where May used to hang photos, he'd had a moment of longing for the wonderful life he'd had with her. He missed the photos too. They were in a box in the attic. Rosie wasn't the only one who kept things close to her heart and away from prying eyes. But he did have snaps of his family on the sideboard.

He had got over losing May to the point that he could look forward and make decisions about where he wanted to be in a few years' time, but he was still vulnerable to memories of the past, and his fear for the future and what might lie ahead if he decided to get involved with another woman. He didn't want to go through anything like the pain he'd felt over losing May, and the guilt that went with it. That had taken everything away from him, especially the ability to make decisions involving his future and he was still a long way from getting that back.

'Coffee is served.' Rosie placed a steaming mug in front of him and sat down on one of the deck chairs with another in her hand. 'This is the life,' she murmured.

She made it all sound so easy. Except he knew it wasn't for her any more than him. Last night would stay with her for a while to come as she recovered from the mental side of being assaulted. He'd do all he could to be there and help her through the worst moments.

It was a sudden decision, but one he had no intention of changing his mind about. Everyone needed a trustworthy person in their life, and he could be that person for Rosie. It wouldn't be about a joint future; it would simply be about helping her get back on her feet to face her own again without images of what happened last night taking away her confidence. Time would show he intended sticking around for a while. Maybe along the way he'd get up to speed with making some decisions about his own future.

CHAPTER THREE

'YOU CAN'T COME back to work until Tuesday at the earliest,' Rosie's boss said.

'Steve, there's nothing wrong with me apart from a few bruises. It's the weekend so I can take it easy and be ready to do anything come Monday.'

She didn't want to sit at home with nothing to occupy her mind, otherwise the time would be filled with images of that evil man laughing at her as he grabbed her bag and hit her, sending her tumbling to the ground. So why had she spent so much time thinking about Lucas when her assailant wasn't taking over? Why was she seeing Lucas in a different way now to when she'd known him before? A few too many hours stood between when she'd been attacked and now for her to keep blaming the assailant for her distracting thoughts of Lucas.

Work was the only answer to her problems.

'Put your doctor hat on,' Steve growled. 'You'll feel sore and stiff for the next few days.

You rarely take time off, apart from the days on the roster, so it won't hurt to use up some of your leave.' He got to his feet. 'I'm serious, Rosie.'

She stood up too, wincing when a stab of pain sliced through her hip. 'So am I, Steve. I can do your paperwork and you can take my place on the chopper, if you like.'

He shook his head firmly. 'I saw that wince, Rosie. You're hurting more than you're letting on. Take Monday off and we'll talk again on Monday night.' He leaned in and gave her a brief hug. 'Take care of yourself. No one deserves what that man did to you. I was really shocked when I got the call from your friend last night. I didn't sleep well.'

'You and me both.' She sighed. 'All right, I'll start back on Tuesday. In the air or at your desk, I don't mind. It's only that I'm worried about having too much spare time on my hands at the moment.'

With spare time came too much thinking about things best left alone. Last night had underlined that running solo wasn't as great as she pretended. There'd been no one to call who'd drop everything to be by her side. Kelly or Simone would have come as they were her best friends, but they both had responsibilities to their own families and that wasn't the same as having her own partner rushing to be with her. Had the time come to start thinking about finally letting a man in, and not keep pushing them away? Lucas? She gasped. But why not? She knew him well enough to know he wouldn't walk away, taking her heart with him. *And* it was a big plus that he'd been there for her last night and this morning. There was more to him than she'd ever considered, which was frightening given how her priority was always to protect herself from being hurt.

'Rosie? Everything all right?'

No. She was having the strangest thoughts about a man she'd only ever known as a friend. A very good-looking friend… 'I'm fine.'

'Call on your pals to drop by. They'll keep you busy talking and laughing.' He'd met Kelly and Simone at her recent thirty-fourth birthday party.

'I was about to email everyone to let them know what happened.' Steve had turned up within minutes of Lucas leaving so there hadn't been time to do anything about informing people of her predicament. 'I need to get onto the insurance company ASAP.' She should've used Lucas's phone while he was here. To think she'd often wondered why anyone had a landline these days. The answer had come hard and fast.

'Want me to hang around so you can use mine to call them? I can let Pam know I'll be a little while.'

Rosie couldn't do that to Pam when Steve was so often away, working or taking work calls at home.

'Thanks, but I'll be fine. I'll use one of the girls' phones when they arrive.' Because there'd be no keeping Kelly and Simone away once they read her email. 'Go have lunch with Pam and forget all about work for an hour.'

When Rosie closed the door behind Steve she sagged back against the wall. Her head pounded. Lucas turning up in her life again was almost as shocking as the assault. In a totally different way, of course, but just as overwhelming. Maybe even more so because she suspected these new feelings weren't going to disappear in a hurry, if at all. It was strange how differently she saw him now. Sucking in a long breath, she wandered into the kitchen. Perhaps because three years had elapsed since he'd lost May? But she had no idea if he'd moved on or not. Nor was she going to do anything to spoil what they already had, a solid friendship that just needed renewing again.

Another coffee while sitting out on the deck might help calm her addled brain. Or not. With her head still aching and her body painful in numerous places, stretching out on the outdoor divan was so tempting, but she doubted her brain would stop bringing up subjects she'd prefer to ignore. Plus, if she didn't get on with letting her nearest and dearest know the score, then once they did find out they'd all be around here reading the riot act for not saying anything. Opening her laptop, she sat uncomfortably at the table and tapped onto her email site. This wouldn't take long. She'd copy in everyone and keep the outline short.

Except typing the details got increasingly more difficult as unwanted images filled her head that definitely had nothing to do with Lucas and made her angry and upset. Once again she was seeing that hideous laughing face, those saucer-sized eyes, and hearing the spin of car wheels on the tarmac. Her fingers shook and too often missed the keys she needed to make sense of what she was trying to tell everyone. Tears spurted out of her eyes.

'Damn you!' she shouted and slammed her fist on the table top. 'Who do you think you are to assault me and steal my bag? Huh? Just who are you?'

Prodding 'send' hard, she shoved the laptop to the middle of the table and dropped her head onto her arms. 'What gave you the right to do this to me?' What he'd done was unbelievable.

Her shoulders heaved as the tears flowed. The attack felt unreal. But it had been real. Which made her feel utterly alone. She wasn't, of course. Steve had not long left. She had friends and her brother to call on, and Lucas was back in her life, but this was different somehow. She'd been through something none of them had and therefore they wouldn't quite understand how it made her feel so useless. Vulnerable. Unable to protect herself. Something she'd spent her life working hard to make sure she was always capable of. Growing up without her mother to love her, and an emotionally distant father, she'd learned early on how other people could hurt her.

Yet now, after one fist to her arm and a speeding car tossing her aside, she felt so uneasy it was horrible. Her heart hadn't been involved. The man was a stranger to her. Yet he'd managed to pull the ground out from under her. Literally and mentally.

But crying wasn't going to improve a thing.

Straightening up, she blew her nose on a handful of tissues and looked around her home. It was hers, and no one could change that. But then, that was what she'd believed about going to shop for groceries yesterday. Her decision, her right, her way. Bang. Changed in a flash.

Ding-dong. Her doorbell. Who could it be? It was too soon after sending the email for it to be any of her friends. There really wasn't anyone else she wanted to talk to, unless it was her brother. As long as he didn't raise the topic of his wedding and her partner, that was. It could be Lucas, but he'd likely be busy with his chores, plus he hadn't long left here. Nor was it fair to put pressure on him when they'd only just caught up, by wanting him here with her. She had no idea where he was at with his life. Despite the time he'd spent with her, he might have a new woman for all she knew. Her stomach sank further. She needed to find out sooner rather than later, then she could either squash these feelings or do something about them. She shook her head. As if she'd ever do that. Better to keep Lucas as a friend than lose him altogether.

The bell rang again.

Sighing, Rosie pushed herself out of the chair and headed to the door. 'Hello?'

'Rosie, it's Megan, the policewoman from last night. Can I come up?'

What? And go through what happened yet again? No, thank you. But then talking about it all in a steady, unemotional way might be the best option she had right now. Before she could overthink it, she pressed the button to let Megan into the building.

'Level three, apartment three.' On the corner so that she had one-eighty-degree views to enjoy when she was in the mood. Not today.

Late afternoon, Lucas reached the main entrance to Rosie's apartment block just as two worried-looking women turned up behind him, carrying flowers and a bottle of wine.

'I hope she's all right,' one of them said in a loud voice. 'She didn't mention any wounds, but Rosie would downplay anything that happened to her.'

'Calm down, Kelly. We don't want her seeing us stressed to the max when she's been through hell.'

Lucas hesitated about pressing the buzzer. These women were obviously friends of Rosie's. She might think two visitors were more than enough. But he hadn't stopped worrying about her all day and wanted to check that she was doing okay. He couldn't walk away without seeing her, however briefly. She'd got to him in a way he hadn't expected, which came as a shock considering he hadn't thought he was anywhere near ready to move on with his life and get out of the hole he'd buried himself in. The guilt kept reminding him he wasn't to be trusted with another woman's heart.

'Excuse me. Can you push star number three for us?' the second woman asked.

'I was about to do that myself,' he said, sounding out their reaction to him.

'You're going up to Rosie's?'

'I was, but if you're doing the same I can come back later.'

Both women were staring at him, small smiles on their faces. 'Hell, no. We'll all go up. You do know what happened to her, don't you?'

Lucas thought about how much to say.

'I'm Simone, by the way, and this is Kelly. We're Rosie's besties, if people our age are allowed to call ourselves that.' Simone laughed. Then her face straightened again. 'Sorry, this isn't the time to be joking.'

'I think you'll find that Rosie would like a few laughs at the moment.'

'So you do know what happened,' said Kelly.

He sighed. 'I was the doctor who saw her when she was brought into the ED yesterday. We used to know each other when we were doing our specialty training a few years back,' he added in case they thought he was being creepy by turning up here. 'Lucas Tanner.'

The women gave each other a nod he couldn't interpret, and Kelly said, 'Press the buzzer. We've got a friend to cheer up.'

A friend who looked as though she could do with some company, Lucas thought as he followed the women into the apartment. There were circles under Rosie's eyes and tension in her shoulders that hadn't been there earlier, probably brought on by too much time alone filled with thoughts of the assault.

'Hey, Rosie, you look like you've gone a round

in the boxing ring,' Simone said as she leaned in and gave Rosie a gentle hug with one arm. 'You all right?'

'I'm fine, though a bit tired.'

'Here's something to cheer you up.' Simone handed her the flowers.

'You didn't have to do that.' Rosie blinked and buried her face in the roses.

'How about this then?' Kelly waved the wine in front of her. 'Then there's your doc friend we found on the steps.'

Rosie glanced at him with a wry grin. 'You'll regret coming up here with these two. They never know when to shut up.'

Which could be a good thing, considering how you might need to be distracted from the images that are no doubt continuously flitting through your mind.

'I'll cope,' he said.

'So, coffee? Or wine?' Kelly asked. She looked to Rosie. 'Or are you drugged up on painkillers?'

'Haven't had any since first thing this morning.'

Lucas sent her a sharp look, which she ignored. He'd bet her hip and thigh were giving her even more grief after kneeling down to help that young woman with the smashed shin.

'So that's a yes.' Kelly opened a cupboard and

got out four glasses. 'Lucas? You'll join us?' She was already pouring the first glass.

'Thanks, but I'll be boring and stick to coffee,' Lucas replied.

Rosie made a move towards the coffee machine.

'I'll make it, Rosie. I've got one of these machines so I know what I'm doing.' He really should've turned around and gone away when he knew Kelly and Simone were visiting her. It was a bit crowded in here with the women bustling around. They seemed to gobble up all the air with their laughter and talk, trying to downplay their concern for Rosie.

He was seeing another side to Rosie he'd forgotten about—her complete relaxation around those she trusted. Not many people, if he remembered correctly, and he had to admit he could've got that one wrong because back then he'd mostly been focused on May and the state of their marriage. He glanced at Rosie. Why had she and Cameron split up? They'd been happy together and seemed on course for marriage and family.

He shook his head. Why did life get messed up so often? It wasn't always wonderful, for sure, and now he'd reconnected with Rosie he had no intention of losing her again. It would be worse this time because he was running solo and that had its lonely moments. So, was he thinking Rosie could fill those? As a friend? Or was he looking for more? No, only as a friend. For now, at least. A shiver ran down his back, making him wonder if he was trying to fool himself.

'Fill us in on everything,' he heard Simone say and he concentrated on that and not what was going on in his head. Then Simone shook her head. 'Sorry, that was a dumb thing to say. I'm sure you don't want to go over the details right now.'

Rosie pulled out a chair at the table and sank onto it, grimacing as if her hip hurt. 'Truth is, I've just spent two hours giving an in-depth statement to one of the policewomen who turned up at the scene yesterday and right now I'm shattered. So, if you don't mind, let's find something else to discuss.'

'Two hours?' Lucas was stunned. 'That seems OTT.'

'Not if they want to nail him in court, apparently.' Rosie sighed. 'The cops have a good idea who attacked me. He did something similar last week to a woman in her eighties. She got a fractured arm when he dragged her along the road with his car for a few metres.'

Lucas felt his heart scrunch. Rosie had got off lightly compared to that, but he was furious all over again. Who did the lowlife think he was, attacking women as if it meant absolutely nothing? About to say something, he glanced at Rosie and kept his mouth shut. She did indeed look exhausted, as if everything was finally catching up big time. It had to happen. He was only surprised it had taken until now, but she had been busy most of the day, what with picking up her car, helping Freya, and giving that statement. He wouldn't stay long. Her friends would make sure she was okay, and she'd probably be more relaxed with them anyway.

'You all right?' he asked quietly.

'We'll make sure she is,' Kelly answered for her.

'Have you had anything to eat since you got home?' Lucas asked.

Her cheeks reddened. 'Not really. I don't feel hungry.'

'I'll make you something. Want a sandwich?'

'That'd be nice. There's cold chicken in the fridge, and some salad in a container.'

'Consider it done.'

Rosie leaned back in her chair, trying to ignore her throbbing hip as she listened to her friends and watched Lucas clean up after he'd made her a sandwich. It was still hard to believe he'd turned up in her life after all this time, and how that had happened. He'd been nothing but supportive since he'd first walked into the cubicle in the ED where the paramedics had deposited her. Friends were the best, she had decided long ago. These two had been with her most of her life, since they'd met at school. Friends didn't turn their backs on her and leave her with a broken heart, like her dad had. What he'd done wasn't usual for a parent, or even a partner. On one level she knew that, but all those years of emotional neglect had affected her so deeply that she just couldn't face being hurt like that again. Lucas would be an amazing friend…only she suspected the warmth she felt for him wasn't only about friendship. And that was dangerous.

The problem was, she'd set herself up to miss out on meaningful relationships because she couldn't face having her heart crushed again. So how come she was looking at Lucas more often than was sensible? Feeling these mixed emotions over him? It was easy to blame the assault for shaking her up, but beginning to understand just what she'd done to herself by remaining so isolated and believing that she was keeping herself safe from heartbreak was more complicated and difficult to ignore. And unusual for her.

'Hey, sleepyhead.' Kelly nudged her. 'You should go lie down for a while.'

Even though she wasn't taking part in the conversation much, she preferred having the company to being on her own. Her friends managed to keep the ghastly memories at bay a little.

'I'm good sitting here, thanks.'

'Have you sorted the problem with Johnno and his wedding yet?' Kelly asked.

'No. The only good thing about not having a phone right now is he can't ring and nag me. I sent him the same email I sent you but chances are he hasn't seen it yet as he and Karen are up in the Yarra Valley this weekend, sorting out seating arrangements and a whole load of other things.'

Johnno would be putting his mate's name on the seat next to hers as she still hadn't come up with an alternative date to accompany her.

'I can think of an answer...' Simone grinned with a slight inclination of her head in Lucas's direction.

'Get out of here,' she muttered.

Simone stood up. 'Actually, I am about to head off now. Toby's taking me out to dinner to celebrate my promotion and I don't want to be late for that.' She was grinning like the cat with the cream.

Glancing at Lucas, Rosie saw him flinch and wondered why. But she couldn't just ignore her friend's excitement. 'Congratulations, Simone! You truly deserve it, you've worked hard enough.' All those long hours at the television station where she worked as a programme organiser had paid off.

'You bet I have.' Then she looked contrite. 'I don't really want to leave you though.'

'I'm fine,' she growled, denying the need to have someone with her for a little longer. Kelly might stay.

Kelly looked from her to Lucas and then to Simone, and grinned. 'I'll come with you. I'm going to Mum and Dad's for tea.' She flicked another look at Lucas as if to say, *Step up, man. She needs you.*

Rosie deliberately looked at the decorative clock on the wall. 'You're going to be late, aren't you?' Considering Kelly's parents had left for Singapore two days ago, she was talking nonsense. These two were stirring up trouble for her, all to do with Lucas.

Her friend just laughed. 'Probably.'

Lucas looked at all three of them and finally said, 'I'll hang out here for a while longer if you can put up with me, Rosie.' He said it with a knowing smile, as if he suspected the girls were setting him up and didn't give a damn.

Thankfully, she hadn't shared their enthusiasm—or her own—or he'd probably have been long gone, especially if he knew what was going on in her head.

'Thanks, Lucas, but I'm sure I can manage.

It's not as though I'm going to be doing anything too strenuous. Might look into what's required to get a pilot's licence.' That had come out of nowhere. It had only been an idea simmering in the back of her mind, not a definite plan. Yet now she knew for sure she was going to do it. Yesterday had been a wakeup call, shown her that she'd never know what might be thrown at her so why keep putting off doing the things she wanted?

'You want to learn to fly?' Lucas looked surprised, also thoughtful.

'I do.' See? She could move forward, stop putting everything on hold, all because she was afraid to lay her heart and soul on the line. A shiver rattled her.

Slow down. You're rushing things.

Wasn't that normal after what had happened to her?

Lucas said, 'Go you. That's brilliant.'

'It sure is,' said Simone, before hugging her. 'See you tomorrow. Look after yourself in the meantime.' She winked.

Maybe it would be good to see the backs of these two as they were nothing if not trouble.

'Check I'm here before you drop by. I might be busy doing something.'

'We have a lunch date, remember?'

'I might change my mind.' No way would she

do that, but perhaps her friends needed reminding they didn't control her life!

All she got in response was more laughter and a hug from Kelly. Then the door shut and the apartment was suddenly quiet.

Rosie leaned back with a sigh. She missed her friends already. Annoying as they could sometimes be, they lit up the room and made her happy.

'You all right?' the remaining person asked again.

'I wish everyone would stop asking me that. I'm a bit sore and stiff, but otherwise I am fine.' Guilt crept in. Lucas didn't deserve her curtness. 'Sorry, Lucas. I know you're just looking out for me, and I really appreciate it.'

'But you'd rather I kept my mouth shut.' He grinned. 'Want to tell me about your problem with your brother's wedding instead?'

Not really, but it was a change of topic and she'd go along with that without saying too much.

'He's getting married in two weeks and wants me to go as his best friend's date. I can't stand the guy so I've refused to oblige, but Johnno is adamant he'll seat us together unless I take someone else who's apparently important to me or that I'm in lust with, or something.'

Why hadn't she found a man to go with?

It wasn't as though she didn't know any single men, and one of them would probably have agreed if she'd asked. But she hadn't been able to get enthused about that idea and hence she was still stuck between a rock and Will Clark.

'The wedding's two weeks away, you say?'

'Yes.'

'How about I go with you? I haven't got anything important on that weekend.'

She stared at Lucas. 'Everyone's going up on Friday and staying two nights.'

'No problem.'

She was still staring. So he had to be single then. 'You're serious? Did you not hear me say I have to at least look like I'm in lust with my date?' Her cheeks were heating up fast. Hopefully, no one would think she found Lucas as attractive as she did. How could she agree to him going without making an idiot of herself? Impossible.

'It's just a suggestion,' Lucas said reasonably. 'A friend helping another friend.'

Had he noticed the smug looks her *friends* had been exchanging before they'd left? If so, what was he thinking?

'I didn't mention we're staying overnight at the vineyard where the wedding's being held. We'd have to share a room.' With one bed most likely.

'I always thought you never turned your back on a challenge.' There was laughter in his voice, which irked her. Or was that the second challenge he'd just issued? Because if that wasn't one, then what was it?

'You win. I accept your offer.' Somehow, she didn't feel disappointed for giving in. Instead, it was more like excitement filling her, which was crazy. Lucas was a great guy, but she wasn't in lust or anything else with him. Or was she lying to herself about that? Hadn't she been thinking otherwise half the night? 'Are you sure you want to do this?' she pressed because she had no idea where her emotions were at.

'As strange as it may seem, I do. It's an opportunity to spend time with you and catch up on what you've been up to since we all went our own ways three years ago. I know it's going to look like we're a couple.' He highlighted that by flicking his forefingers in air quotes between them. 'But there'll be times when we'll be by ourselves without having to keep alert and can just relax.'

Not play out the 'in lust' part? Was that disappointment? Couldn't be. It was so good to see Lucas again, to have him looking out for her, she was getting carried away.

'You're right. There will be.' Though not many, as there were lots of get-togethers planned for the weekend, which was a shame because she realised she'd like a lot of time with just Lucas to sort out her mixed emotions. 'For the record, I know Johnno only has the best of intentions when it comes to pairing me up with his best friend. He thinks I'm not giving Will enough of a chance, but I haven't told him how rude and arrogant Will was the one and only time I went out with him. I didn't want to make things awkward for my brother.'

'I understand.' Lucas gave her a heart-softening smile. 'So, we're agreed? We're going to the wedding together.'

'Yes, we are.' He'd made it too easy for her to accept. Only yesterday the idea of asking Lucas to accompany her had popped into her startled mind and she'd kicked it out fast. Now she was good with the idea, though she wasn't going to think about sharing a room and therefore a bed with him. That was too much to take in right now. 'There's a dinner on the Friday night for Karen's and Johnno's families. As my partner, you'll be a part of that.' Last chance for him to bail.

'Of course.' Lucas looked thoughtful. 'Are we really going to be able to fool Johnno that we're in lust with each other? If you haven't come up with a date until now, he's going to know you weren't asking anyone else.'

'True.' Did Lucas think she was pathetic not having a man in her life, one she could've invited to the wedding anyway? 'Johnno knows I shy away from relationships and thinks I need a helping hand finding someone.' She closed her eyes. She'd gone too far. Now Lucas would be thinking the same. 'I sound pathetic, I know.'

A warm hand covered hers. 'We're two peas in a pod.'

'What?' Her eyes flew open. 'You do the same?' At least he had good reason to keep to himself. He'd lost the woman he loved. She'd lost her mother, and then her father's love. Same, but not the same.

'Yes, Rosie, I do.' He withdrew his hand and stood up to go get two wine glasses and open a bottle she had in the fridge. Handing her a glass, he said, 'Here, relax. Your wedding problem is solved.'

'Thanks.' She'd barely touched the wine Kelly had poured her and Simone had finished it off.

Sitting on the couch opposite, he breathed deeply. 'Losing May crippled me,' he stated bluntly.

'Of course it did.'

Leaning forward, elbows on his knees, he studied the floor. 'I don't know if or when I'll ever be able to move on after what happened. Will I ever reach that point?' He paused for a moment. Talking about this couldn't be easy. Yet he seemed determined to tell her where he was at. 'I have no idea what lies ahead for me in terms of another long-term relationship. I only know I'm not ready to find out yet.'

Internally, Rosie slumped. Outwardly, she worked hard at not showing that his admission rattled her when she should be relieved that she could put away these strange feelings of need and desire and get on with recovering from the attack instead of thinking Lucas might've come back into her life for a special reason.

'I suppose only time will tell,' she murmured, knowing she'd let him down with such an inane comment. But she had to protect herself too.

'So I've often heard.' His smile was crooked. 'But it's okay. If I don't know, how can anyone else?'

She could relate to that, after years of waiting for her dad to return to being the father he once was. Then a thought struck her hard. Neither she nor Lucas were truly available to put their hearts on the line. Was she relieved or not?

'We'll have a fun, friendly weekend. Thanks to you, my problem is solved.'

'Do you need to tell Johnno while he's up in the Yarra Valley?'

'You're way ahead of me. I'll email him now.' Reaching for her laptop, she opened up the email site and began composing a message, ignoring the slight shake in her fingers. Lucas was going to the wedding with her. What had she let herself in for? A lot of fun? Or more problems at a time she didn't need them? Go with the fun. Much better, and it might even lead to more good times. Except neither of them was emotionally available, remember? Therein lay the problem. She was such a worrywart.

Her glass appeared on the small table beside her. 'Get some of this into you and stop overthinking it all. Things will work out.'

'I hope so.' No, damn it, she'd make sure they had a great time without getting carried away.

She was confident about looking out for herself, but not about letting a man in to do that for her and steal her heart at the same time. Lifting her glass, she tapped it against Lucas's. 'It is so good to find you again. Given that you're working in Parkville, it was only a matter of time before we came across each other in the ED, but I'm really glad it's already happened.'

'Back at you.' Lucas settled into an armchair beside her. 'I've often wondered where everyone's living and working, what they're up to. Married, family, the mortgage. All that sort of stuff. I keep in touch with Brett. He wouldn't let me walk away when I left Melbourne, insisted we stay in contact, and I'm glad he did. I needed that. He's now working in Sydney, but he came over to San Fran to catch up a couple of times. We went off on treks in national parks both times.'

'Laurie's in Perth, married to an awesome guy who's a nurse. They've got two toddlers, and she works part-time in an emergency department. I heard Nathan's living in London, working at one of the bigger hospitals. Whether he's married or not I have no clue.'

'That's the whole team accounted for, then.'

'It felt weird when we first went our separate ways. No one to vent to about a particularly bad day. We had a special bond back then.'

'Before it all blew up in our faces.'

Rosie grabbed his hand. 'We missed you when you left after May died. It was such a dreadful time. Everyone felt for you and would've done anything to go back to before it happened.' Which was the understatement of the year. They'd all felt guilty for not being able to help Lucas through his pain, and when he'd left Melbourne it had seemed even worse, as if they'd failed big time even though they knew he'd left not only them but his family and other friends to put space between everyone and himself.

'You'd have had to have been queued up behind me to do that.'

The sadness in Lucas's face told her how much

he still carried the weight from that night. Right from the moment he'd learned that May had died he'd blamed himself for being at work instead of being in the car with her when she'd spun it out and slammed into a concrete wall. But it hadn't been his fault. He was a doctor through to his bones and couldn't have left a dying patient. But she knew from experience not to say that to him. He'd only tell her she had no idea what she was talking about, and maybe he was right. She had her own experience of losing people she loved, albeit in very different circumstances.

'I'm not surprised.'

They sat quietly, lost in their own thoughts, until Lucas finally said, 'Want me to sort something for dinner, or would you like some time to yourself?'

'If you want to hang around, then that'd be great.' She still wasn't ready to be alone with all those images from yesterday. Now she could add new, better ones about Lucas joining her for her brother's wedding, but she wasn't so sure she wanted to be inundated with those either. Lucas had admitted he wasn't over May, so she had to concentrate on remaining friends. Coming up with any number of images involving him was off-limits. 'My head's a mess, to put it bluntly.' When he started to laugh, she held up her hand. 'Stop. I'm not talking about the bruises.'

'I know that.' His laughter died away. 'It's going to take time to get over what happened.'

But I've got you to help me through it.

'Not too long. I refuse to let him win on that score.'

'Now there's a surprise.'

'Why did I offer to go to the wedding?' Lucas wondered out loud. It was another way to help Rosie out, but sharing a hotel room? A bed? When he was all over the place about what he might want from her.

'Absolutely bonkers, that's what I am.' Except there was a new bounce in his step as he walked back to his house from her apartment. The air felt lighter and the sky was shining. 'Yeah, I am totally losing the plot.'

Which went to show how much Rosie had got to him in a very short time. Not a lot more than twenty-four hours ago she hadn't been in his life and yet now here he was thinking he'd like to get to know her better. She was already starting to feel special to him.

But enough to share a whole weekend away with her?

He grinned as warmth stole under his ribs. Yeah, why not?

If it turned out he was wrong about the excitement he felt around Rosie then at least he'd have an answer. The chances were high for that to happen as he still felt he wasn't ready to engage in a full-time relationship, not even with a beautiful and wonderful woman like Rosie. The guilt and sadness over May's death still filled his heart and wouldn't be disappearing any time soon as far as he could tell.

But he couldn't help thinking he'd love to get to a deeper level than casual friends with Rosie. Was he ready for that, if nothing else? He guessed the weekend away could answer that.

CHAPTER FOUR

'CHOPPER'S FIVE MINUTES AWAY,' Chris told Lucas.

'Let's get up to the helipad now.' It was Thursday afternoon and the ED was having a quiet time, as in not every bed was full and the waiting room only had two people needing to be seen by a doctor as soon as one was free. 'I want to be there before they touch down.'

From what the Life Flight caller had said, a man had fallen off the fourth floor of a building on a construction site and was bleeding extensively, internally and externally. He'd need all the help they could give him and some. A general surgeon and an orthopaedic specialist were on standby with a theatre ready and waiting.

As soon as the chopper landed and the door began opening Lucas made his way across to collect their patient.

Rosie appeared in the doorway, looking calm and in control, though that was probably a lie. No one could be in control of what was going on with the man with his extensive injuries.

'Hey, Lucas, Chris, we need this man in Theatre ASAP. I suspect pneumothorax. We've got an oxygen tube in but it's not looking good.'

'On it.' Within minutes he and Chris were pushing the trolley towards the door to go inside, while a nurse from the chopper held the heart monitor steady.

Beside him, Rosie was filling in the details. 'Trent suffered cardiac arrest fifteen minutes ago. Due to blood loss, I'd say. His heart rate's low. I expect another arrest any moment. Both legs have multiple fractures, likewise both arms. There's a contusion on his skull even though he wore a hard hat.'

The heart monitor flatlined.

'Here we go.' Rosie was already reaching for the defibrillator. 'Stand back everyone.'

The man's body jerked upward, sank back down.

The line on the monitor remained flat.

Lucas cursed under his breath. Compressions were out, due to the lung damage. *Hurry up, defib.*

'Stand back.'

Another electric current lifted the man's body, and this time the line moved upward.

Lucas felt no relief. There was a long way to go before Trent was out of danger. 'Move it. Fast as possible.'

The four of them focused on speed without causing further stress to their patient. Once in the ED, Rosie handed over notes and swapped over the defib for the hospital one by the bed.

'How long was Trent on the ground before medical help arrived?' Lucas asked her after telling Chris to let the surgeons on standby know their patient was in the ED.

She didn't stop what she was doing as she answered. 'An ambulance was there fifteen minutes after he fell. We were approximately another fifteen minutes after that. He wasn't brought in by road because of the peak-hour traffic.'

Lucas winced. It was a fast pickup, but still a long time when Trent was bleeding out.

'Trent's been unconscious the whole time. Observers say he took the brunt of the fall on his legs. The worst bleeding is coming from his chest. While the suspected pneumothorax is the greatest source of blood loss, I think he's also haemorrhaging in the abdominal region,' she said.

He was already checking the abdomen and coming to the same conclusion. 'I agree.'

'Heart rate's dropping,' a nurse warned.

'Get ready for another shock if needed,' he warned, even though it was already under control. Where the hell were the surgeons? The man wouldn't be able to take much more. Of course the specialists would be on their way, be here any second, but he hated these moments when most things were out of his hands except trying to keep the patient alive. They couldn't stop the bleeding in the lungs by applying pressure as that'd only push the broken ribs in deeper and cause more trouble.

'Lucas, I've got you.' Aaron, the general surgeon on standby, appeared at his side. 'Fill me in,' he said, already feeling around Trent's ribcage.

The other surgeon arrived at the other side of the bed.

Lucas nodded to Rosie. 'You fill them in.'

With a grim nod, she told the surgeons all she could about Trent's injuries.

'Right, let's get to Theatre and start putting him back together,' Aaron said.

Lucas sighed with relief. No one was wasting time. 'Keep me posted.'

When he looked around after Trent had been taken away, Rosie was nowhere to be seen. Disappointment snagged at him. But then why would she still be here? She had a job to do and that wasn't in the ED but back out amongst the busy city environs or further beyond in the countryside. He'd liked working alongside her as they got Trent's heart up and running. She was calm, focused, and didn't mess about.

Now that the case was out of his hands he was beginning to sag mentally. He didn't have to remain on edge in case he got something wrong or something else happened to Trent that caused more problems. Right then he made up his mind to call Rosie when he signed off and suggest they go somewhere for a drink to ease all the work tension.

He also wanted to catch up on how she was doing, both physically and mentally. She'd called him on Monday night to say she'd replaced her phone and arranged for new bank cards. He hadn't trusted her chirpy manner as he felt she might've been putting on a show to keep him at arm's length. It was time to stop holding back whenever he was worried about her. They were closer than that. Especially now they were going away for a weekend together.

'Sorry I'm late, but we had to pick up a child from Yarra Valley. She'd dived into the school swimming pool and hit her head on the bottom.' Rosie sank onto the stool at the table Lucas had claimed and huffed out a long breath, ridding herself of some of the tension in her shoulders, glad Lucas had suggested meeting up after work. 'What a day. How's Trent doing?'

'I'll fill you in after I've got you a drink.'

'Good man. Wine would be awesome.' It

might even help her sleep tonight. There were some nights after distressing times with patients when sleep could be elusive to the point she'd be lucky to get a couple of hours. Bad cases always weighed heavily on her mind as she questioned whether she could have done things differently to get a better outcome. Along with working hard to save Trent, today's last case had been one of those. The little girl had been pulled unconscious from the pool by a parent. The head injury was severe, her lungs full of water and, from what Rosie ascertained, very likely her neck was broken too.

'Here, get that into you. You look like you're about to fall apart.' Lucas pushed a glass in front of her. 'I take it things don't look good for the young girl?'

Rosie's own neck ached as she nodded. 'Not at all.'

'Well, Trent's conscious now and fairly lucid. The hard hat saved him from serious brain trauma. Plus the fact he took the brunt of the fall on his legs.' Lucas drank a deep mouthful of beer. 'Therein ends the good news.'

'His legs are in a bad way?'

'It's unlikely he'll get full use of them back. Both lungs were perforated, and his liver needed sectioning.' The saddest emotions filled Lucas's face. 'It's one of those days when I wonder why I didn't become a truck driver.'

Shuffling her stool closer to him, she took his hand in hers. 'It's never too late to change careers. I could be your offsider so you don't have to park up when your hours behind the wheel run out.' It felt so good to be here with Lucas, her hand around his in an entirely friendly way. They understood each other and how their day had affected them as non-medical friends wouldn't.

He choked out a laugh. 'I remember the time you said you'd become a barber and shave all your clients' heads bald.'

'I don't remember that. It seems a bit extreme, even for me.'

'You'd seen a man with melanomas on his scalp that had only been found when he decided to get his long hair shaved off to raise money for a charity.'

Rosie thought back to that time. 'I still don't recall saying it, but my reaction does make sense now.'

'He'd come to town to see his girlfriend and when he got to her house she didn't recognise him. Or so the story went in the local rag.' Lucas grinned and reached for his beer again.

Slipping her hand away, she picked up her glass too, this time taking a small sip, her mind busy flipping through previous times when those available in their group got together. 'I remember when Brett said he was going to take up ironing for a living, starting with his own shirts as his current girlfriend was useless at it.'

Lucas grinned. 'I remember that too. The girlfriend didn't take kindly to what Brett said and told him he could cook dinner every night for the next month, which I think he did whenever he wasn't on night shift. He must've been in lust at the time.'

In lust. Rosie smiled to herself. That sounded like fun with no hitches. But not what she was getting into with Lucas, because something told her it wouldn't stop at that—if anything ever happened between them, which it couldn't. Right now, her hand felt warm where it had touched his skin in a way that had nothing to do with letting go of the day and more to do with how attracted she was to him. It was great sitting here laughing about nothing when both of them had had an awful day, but this connection between them was also getting a little more intense than she was prepared for.

'It's been a long time since I've been able to offload to someone like this.'

'Know what you mean. It was one of the things I missed when I headed away from Melbourne. Though I was usually struggling too much with losing May to be stressing about a bad day in the ED.' He forced a smile. 'Let's not go there tonight.'

Fair enough. They were here to destress from a bad day, not add to it.

'Why did you opt for San Francisco? I'd have thought you'd go to a smaller town.' He'd used to say when he'd finished training that he'd like to move to a town on the coast where he didn't have to grapple with traffic and lots of people every time he went shopping. Then she remembered he'd signed up for a position in Melbourne's CBD before his life went pear-shaped. Something to do with the house he and May were going to do up.

'Cities are more impersonal. I didn't have to deal with kind and caring people wanting to know too much about my past.'

Ouch. That wasn't good.

'That's sad. You were always very sociable.'

'Only because May had my back. Until I met her, I was quite introverted, stayed in the background a lot. We met in our first year at university and were together from then on.'

'Wow, that's special.'

He nodded. 'It was. Back to why San Fran. I had a friend at school who came from there so I always had an interest in the place. His dad was Aussie and his mum was from California. While

I was there, he came across to visit relations a couple of times and we'd catch up.'

'You mentioned hiking. That must've been fun.'

'There were moments when I wondered if I was mad, but mostly it was challenging and exciting. I also took up cycling as it was a great way to get around the city.'

She could just imagine those long legs pedalling away while his upper body hunched over the front of the cycle. Odd how she was noticing his physical attributes when once she wouldn't have looked at him twice in that way. Not often anyway. He was good-looking as well as tall and muscular. Her type for sure. Gulp.

Grabbing her glass, she tipped her head back and took a large mouthful of wine. Then, putting it down, she made to stand up.

'You suddenly in a hurry to go?'

Yes. I need to put space between us while I clear my head of these out-of-order thoughts.

Before she could come up with a reasonable excuse, Lucas said, 'Let's grab a bite to eat while we're here.'

She hesitated. Despite these unusual sensations, she liked being with Lucas. He was easy to get along with and had no expectations other than to enjoy her company. He didn't appear to be looking for more than friendship.

'No more talk about today or the past,' he added.

Was he lonely too?

'Good idea. The food, I mean,' she added. She hadn't thought she was too lonely, but after Lucas had spent time with her last weekend she'd begun to think it was fun having someone to do things like this with. Kelly and Simone were often in and out of her days but they both had husbands who naturally came first. Then she shook her head as another thought struck. 'I haven't told you. Last night, the police arrested the guy who attacked me. He's behind bars for now at least.'

Lucas was on his feet, coming around the table to wrap her in his arms. 'That's the best news I've heard all day. Probably longer.'

Pressing in against him, she agreed. 'I can relax now. He's not going to find me and have another crack.'

Lucas leaned back so he could see her face, still holding her. 'Were you worried about that? It was very unlikely.'

'I know, but my head's been in some strange places lately.'

'I bet.' He stepped away, taking those comforting arms with him.

She sank onto her stool. 'Now the fun really starts, according to Megan—the cop,' she added, in case Lucas had forgotten her name. 'She warned me that getting a sentence isn't straightforward unless he steps up and admits everything he did, which includes a stolen vehicle, stolen number plates, drug paraphernalia in the car, et cetera.'

'But he'll remain locked up in the meantime?'

'Yes. He's got a history of similar crimes.' She shuddered at the thought of what else he could've done to her.

'Best they throw away the key.' He made this easier to face with his straightforward approach.

'I agree.' Picking up her glass, she said, 'I'm going to have another wine.' She only had a little way to walk home. 'Want any more beer?'

'What sort of question's that?'

Her grin widened. All because Lucas had her back. 'I'll grab some menus.' She picked up his empty glass and headed to the bar, feeling a little light-headed. She couldn't believe they'd talked about the day and come through laughing—just like old times, only better.

She was struggling to comprehend how much Lucas was lighting her up on the inside. He was something else, with that toned body and warm chocolate-brown eyes that saw too much. Not that she minded, as she hadn't given away anything about herself she didn't want him knowing. So far, anyway. To think they were going to Johnno's wedding together. That excited her. To have a date who wasn't Will made all the difference to her feelings about the wedding, even though Lucas would only be playing a role. So would she. She'd have to be careful not to overstep the mark with Lucas and have him wishing he hadn't offered to accompany her.

She'd never intended avoiding the wedding because of Will. She was Johnno's only family and she'd be there for him, no matter what else was going on. His fiancée, Karen, was gorgeous and perfect for him. Fingers crossed he didn't stuff up this time and leave her, as he did his first wife. Johnno's insecurities about love and relationships were as bad as hers, Rosie conceded. While she never lasted long with a man, Johnno went further like getting married, and then started looking for problems that weren't necessarily there. This time, Rosie intended keeping an eye on him and talking to him before it was too late, and not after everything went belly-up.

'As if I know what the hell I'm talking about,' she muttered as she placed the glasses on the bar. Why had their father withdrawn his loving side all those years ago? She'd lost count of how many times she'd asked herself that. There'd never been an answer, even when she'd asked her father directly on the day she'd left home to go to university. He'd shaken his head silently and gone out to the shed to chop firewood.

'Another wine and beer?' the woman behind the counter asked as she put their glasses in the washer.

'Thanks, and menus.' Time to stop being so glum when she was having fun. Lucas might change his mind about going to the wedding if she didn't.

'Order me the medium rare steak and chips,' Lucas told her when she returned to their table with the menus.

'You've been here before.'

'Often.'

'Me too, I'm surprised we didn't bump into each other here before.' She put the menus aside and went to order their meals and fetch their fresh drinks.

Lucas watched Rosie weave her way through the tables towards him, fighting the wave of longing swamping him. She was gorgeous. He had noticed before, of course, but purely objectively.

Because I loved May.

True. But now? Had the time finally come to move on, maybe with Rosie? The constrictions around his heart were loosening. But it wouldn't be easy to adjust to this new state. He was still afraid to give his heart away again. Nor had the guilt over the accident that took May from him vanished. Not at all.

If they hadn't argued that night, May would still be here. The disc with that refrain went round and round in his head. If he hadn't stayed back at work to save the life of a man who was bleeding out on the ED floor, May would still be with him.

Yeah, and if May hadn't told him her promotion meant moving to Sydney in a fortnight he wouldn't have got angry and they wouldn't have had that fierce argument, and she mightn't have said he was selfish and she was going to Sydney whether he decided to join her there or not. Put bluntly, she'd told him they were over unless he agreed to her demands. Demands that scrubbed him raw because they'd been on the same page when they'd bought their first house with the idea of living in Melbourne for the next few years.

'Here, get that into you and put a smile back on your face.' Rosie placed a beer in front of him. 'You look like you need cheering up.'

He did, but it was up to him to get over what had spoiled his mood. Digging deep, he leaned close and said, 'I know the circumstances were awful for you, but I'm glad we've caught up again. It's great seeing you and doing things like this.'

'I totally agree. Catching up with you has made me realise how much I've missed the group too.'

Missed the group? Not just him? That put him in his place. He pulled back and sipped his beer, but not before a heady scent of roses teased him. That was something else he didn't recall from the past. He probably wouldn't have noticed Rosie's perfume then, but now he had it wasn't disappearing in a hurry. So he breathed deep and made the most of the lovely scent. A bit like he was doing sharing this evening with Rosie herself. Making the most of everything.

They were soon going to spend a weekend together. As friends, nothing else, he reminded himself for the umpteenth time since first offering to go to the wedding with her. Except Rosie needed him to look keen on her to keep her brother's friend at arm's length. Could prove interesting. On all fronts, not least being close to Rosie without getting too intense. Interesting or difficult? Time would answer that.

'Lucas. You still with me?'

More than you would guess.

'I take it we have to be dressed to the nines for the wedding?'

He might have to go shopping for a suit and shirt. These days, he wasn't into shopping for fancy clothes but this could be fun. He could deck himself out to look good for Rosie. He grinned. That was a first in too long. Dressing up in decent gear used to be enjoyable.

'Yes, we do. Karen's parents have gone all-out to make this a luxury wedding. She's their only child and they want the best for her.'

'Why did your face drop when you said that?' Was Rosie jealous? Of course her parents weren't around to do something like that for her, but still.

'Johnno isn't into stable relationships, and tends to leave too quickly if the smallest thing goes wrong. This is his second marriage. I worry for him and Karen.'

'There's not a lot you can do but be there when he needs someone to talk to. He does talk to you?' She'd said Johnno was always there for her, but that didn't mean it worked in reverse.

'He's learning to. Takes a bit of effort, but I can be a nag when necessary.'

'Thanks for the warning.'

Rosie laughed. 'Count yourself lucky we won't be spending a lot of time together or you might get to see me at my worst.'

Not a lot of time together? Yeah, he got that, but it still grated. He wasn't ready to relinquish this bond they were rapidly forming, but he had to be careful. He might feel sparks around her but he had no idea what Rosie thought of him beyond being his friend. Hell, he didn't really know what he thought except he seemed to be falling off the rails when it came to keeping his heart under lock and key.

'I hear you. As for spending time together at the wedding, let me assure you that I will play my role to the full without overdoing it.'

Again, her face looked as if it was about to crumple, then she rallied. 'I'm not looking for anything more than regaining the camaraderie we once had, Lucas. I don't do long-term relationships either.'

Just like her brother? A leftover from growing up without a mother and their father physically present while absent in the loving parent department? The idea made his heart constrict. Rosie deserved better. So did everyone, but he especially wanted it for Rosie. In the short time since they'd reunited, he'd come to enjoy time spent with her and wanted to know her better, and yes, well, just share things with her.

No, I don't.

Yes, he did. Did this mean he truly was beginning to get over what had happened to May? *Was* the guilt quietening down after all this time? That seemed hard to believe when he still felt it was his fault she'd been so angry that she'd driven too fast that night. Of course she'd owned some of the responsibility for the crash that had taken her life, but if he hadn't stayed late at work then chances were high that she wouldn't have dumped her ultimatum on him in the way she had and then sped through the city.

'I hate to say it, but I don't intend settling down with anyone for a long while, if ever.'

'Then we have nothing to worry about next weekend. We can let our hair down, enjoy ourselves while keeping Johnno off my case.'

Again, Lucas felt his heart constricting, which made no sense at all as they were on the same page about this. 'Is the other guy likely to cause any problems now that you're going with me?'

'I doubt it. More likely he'll ignore me so I can realise what I'm missing out on.' Rosie pulled a face. 'That sounded catty, but I told you I don't have pleasant memories of Will.'

The buzzer Rosie had brought back to the table let them know their meals were ready.

'I'll get those.' He needed a break from those beautiful blue eyes that sidetracked his sane and sensible mind whenever they met his.

'I can't believe we live only a few streets apart,' Rosie said as they strolled towards her apartment block.

Was fate playing games with them? Lucas wondered. If so, he didn't mind. 'All I can say is I'm glad it's happened, though again, I would've preferred it to come about some other way.'

'Agreed.'

'Will you go to court to testify if the creep pleads not guilty?'

'Yes, of course. I'll do what it takes to put him behind bars. Megan said they could put up a screen so I don't have to face him, but I said no way. If he goes to trial then I'll stare him down, not let him think he's messed with me so much I can't face him.'

'I'll be there with a noose over my shoulder.' He half meant it.

Rosie laughed at him. 'That doesn't surprise me, but you'd get locked up quicker than him, I reckon.'

'True. Wishful thinking isn't always the brightest.'

She leaned in and rubbed her shoulder against his upper arm. 'Thanks for the offer. I'm not saying it'll be easy, only that I'm determined he's not winning this one.'

Slipping an arm around her waist, he held her lightly. 'Does he still keep you awake at night?'

'Not quite so often now. Where I have more difficulty is busy car parks with cars coming and going. Though not going at the speed he did, they still worry me. I also find myself keeping an eye out for women who leave their handbags or wallets in the grocery trolley while they're putting laden bags into their car. I've stopped and talked to a couple about the risks. They were surprised and then thankful, but whether it'll change anything I have no idea.'

His arm tightened. Rosie was one tough lady, but then he'd said that before.

'There's not a lot else you can do. As long as you're getting the message through to others and helping yourself along the way, then keep doing it.'

Rosie turned and looked at him. 'Thanks for being so supportive. It means a lot.' Then she leaned in and went to touch his cheek with her warm lips.

He turned slightly at the same moment and his mouth ended up on hers, feeling the softness and warmth exuding from her. 'Rosie?' He jerked his head back. 'Sorry. I didn't mean for that to happen.'

Her eyes widened as she stared at him. The tip of her tongue did a lap of her lips.

He couldn't tell if she was disappointed he'd pulled back or taken aback at his mistake. He didn't know how he felt, except it had been an exquisite moment.

'Rosie?'

She blinked. 'Lucas.' Her hand ran down his arm. 'I'd better go inside. We'll talk during the week about the wedding.'

'Nothing's changed on my end,' he said quietly.

'Good. See you.' She flapped a hand at him before spinning around and striding across the road to the apartment building.

Leaving him with a thudding heart and feeling stupid. He had stuffed up big time. He wasn't in the market for a relationship with anyone. But hell, Rosie was something else.

Rosie closed the door and leaned back against it, arms folded across her chest. 'Wow.' The shortest kiss in history and her legs were wonky and her heart almost bursting. 'What happened there?' One moment she was about to brush a light thank you kiss over Lucas's cheek and the next his mouth was on hers, filling her with wonder.

He'd said nothing had changed. Tell that to someone who wasn't getting in a tizz about the sensations his kiss brought on. It wasn't working for her. If he hadn't pulled away when he had there was no accounting for what she might've done next.

Sliding down the door, she sat with her arms tight around her knees. 'Damn you, Lucas.' They'd been getting along so well, and now this. Except she couldn't blame him entirely. She had enjoyed having his mouth on hers, had wanted to deepen the kiss. Only she didn't usually go around kissing her friends. A bitter laugh erupted across her lips. Face it, she didn't kiss anyone much at all.

There hadn't been a man in her life for ages, and that was how she liked it because then no one got hurt. Especially her. Except she was getting tired of running solo. Friends were all very well but there were aspects of being a couple that were missing in friendships. The day-to-day sharing and caring, for one thing. Knowing she had someone to come home to at the end of a gruelling day another. With Kelly and Simone focused on their other halves these days, she was starting to see that she could end up a lonely old woman if she didn't at least try to let go of the fear she had of falling in love, only to withdraw as the relationship intensified.

But how did she do that? It wasn't as if she could just pretend nothing hurt any more and she was free to get on with falling in love with an amazing man and trusting him not to walk away. Trusting him not to break her heart and leave her to go on loving him for ever with no chance of reuniting. Which was why she'd left Cameron. He'd been getting too close and she'd been afraid of where it was going.

Lucas was in her head right now. He was wonderful. She liked him a lot. Liked? Or loved a little bit? Possibly that, she acknowledged, but friends loved each other in a different way to couples. Didn't they? She didn't know the answer to that, having walked away from every relationship she'd been in without her heart even feeling too dented. But then she was good at dampening down any feelings where her heart was concerned. The one lesson her father had taught her too well.

Her phone buzzed.

'Hey, Johnno, how's things?'

'You know what? Really good. I'm so excited about marrying Karen, Rosie. It feels different this time.'

Am I hearing correctly?

'I hope so. She's special and deserves the best from you.'

'I know. She's going to get it. I'm sick of living with the past riding on my shoulders. It's time to let it all go and forget how Dad messed with us.'

Yeah, right. As easy as that—she didn't think. But at least he was trying. Which was more than she was prepared to do.

'Go you.'

'What about you and this Lucas guy you're bringing to the wedding? How's that working out?'

'Wonderful.' If she could stop thinking how his kiss had her in a pickle, wanting more.

'Glad to hear it. I mean it, Rosie. It's time for both of us to have the lives we've always dreamed about. We can't let our family history wreck our futures.'

Thank goodness she was already sitting on the floor or she'd have crash-landed after hearing that. Never, ever, had Johnno said anything remotely close to that before. Why tonight, when Lucas already had her wondering if she could change? When his short kiss had tipped her thinking out of its usual boundaries.

'Johnno, I don't know what to say, other than it's wonderful you feel this way.'

It boded well for his marriage. As long as he kept on track.

'You can do it, too.'

Could she? She wanted to. She did? Of course she did. She'd spent her life denying how much she longed to feel loved and cared about and had instead invested in denying it was possible, yet now Lucas had started changing that. Throw in her brother's comments and it felt too much all of a sudden. She had no idea how to progress from here. It was easier to carry on as she always had, remaining untouchable.

Except she really didn't want to do that any more.

CHAPTER FIVE

'THAT'S THEM,' LUCAS said to the nurse beside him as he pointed to the moving light in the night sky above the hospital. The rescue chopper was bringing them a woman caught in a major house fire. He had a general surgeon on standby, but chances were that wouldn't be enough if the burns were as serious as indicated by the emergency caller.

Vivienne shivered as the air swirled around them as the chopper approached. 'I can't imagine being caught in a fire.'

'Terrifying, to say the least.'

Was Rosie on board? Like him, she was on nights this week. They'd talked on the phone once since he'd kissed her and she'd sounded fine, as though nothing had changed. Something to be grateful for—if he wasn't thinking he might be missing out on a wonderful opportunity to find happiness again.

Tomorrow they were heading north to the Yarra Valley and *that* shared room. Normally, he'd have said 'bring it on' if he was with a hot lady, and he wanted to now but he was wary of getting lost in all the emotions that Rosie engendered within him. Over the last two weeks she'd got to him in ways he hadn't believed possible, tapping into his guilt, his fears of making a mess of loving someone again. Could it be because he'd known her as a friend and therefore felt comfortable to let his guard down with her?

'Here we go.' Vivienne began moving towards the chopper settling on the rooftop.

The door on the side of the aircraft opened and yes, Rosie appeared, hand on the stretcher, ready to roll her patient out.

His heart running faster than normal, Lucas strode across. 'Hey, Rosie. I hear we've got serious burns. I didn't bring a bed up as I don't think it's wise to move the patient any more than absolutely necessary.'

She stepped closer. The scent of roses filled the air. 'Quite agree. We haven't strapped her to the stretcher for the same reason. She's got third-degree burns to arms, shoulders and back. Lesser degree burns on abdomen and upper legs.'

Lucas winced as he began moving the trolley towards the entry door. He couldn't begin to imagine what the woman had been through, let alone what was to come over the weeks and months ahead. 'Is she conscious?'

'Barely. I've got her on oxycodone along with oxygen as her breathing's erratic. Fortunately, her face has no burns so she can wear a mask. She was asleep when her bed caught fire.' Rosie handed him the notes she'd written up. 'Holly Green, early thirties, according to a neighbour. There are two others being taken to another hospital right now.' She drew in a deep breath, then exhaled. 'It's an absolute nightmare for them.'

Lucas touched her hand lightly. 'It sure is. Let's get Holly to the ED.' Rosie would remain with them until they'd got Holly off the stretcher and onto a bed in the high priority room.

Rosie already had one hand on the stretcher. 'I wonder if she's got burns to her lungs.'

'One of the first things I need to find out.' Breathing would be excruciating if that was the case. He got onto the phone as the lift began heading down. 'Geoff, you definitely need to see this patient.' He filled the surgeon in on Holly's condition. 'We're about to roll into the ED now.'

Rosie and Vivienne pushed the trolley carefully, making sure they didn't jar Holly. As soon as they were by the bed, where other staff waited for their patient, Rosie was preparing the woman to be transferred over. Her phone beeped but she ignored it, holding one corner of the board they were sliding Holly onto before shifting her across.

Once they were done, Rosie pulled the phone from her jacket. 'We're on our way up,' she told presumably the pilot. 'Vivienne, we've got another job. I'll call you later in the morning, Lucas.'

He was concentrating on Holly and only said, 'Do that.' She'd understand what was important here. Though last time he'd thought that, May had lost her temper at him and driven into a wall. A shudder ripped through him. Gritting his teeth, he continued assessing the burns in front of him. Right now, Holly was more important than anything else, including his feelings about one certain lady.

But four hours later, when he crawled into bed after a long shower, everything came tumbling back into his head. It was as if he had no control over what he thought about Rosie. That had been a definite wake-up call when he'd thought about May's reaction to him helping a code one patient rather than going home to celebrate with her. No way could he see Rosie losing her temper about that, because she'd be the first to stop and help someone needing her skills.

There was nothing he could do about the past and plenty to make a happy future if he was just willing to give it a chance. Was he? When he still felt so guilty over that night? Would it ever fully go away or was it something he'd have to swallow and deal with whenever it arose? He wasn't even thinking about where their marriage might've been heading at the time. There were no answers to that, though it was unusual he was even thinking this way when, only a few weeks ago, it wouldn't have occurred to him.

Lucas rolled onto his other side and tugged his pillow tight around his neck, closed his eyes and breathed long and slow, willing sleep to come.

Instead, Rosie came skimming though his mind, putting an end to that idea. Her devastating smile. Those sensuous lips he'd felt under his mouth the other night. Her sensational body that melded into him whenever he'd held her. Her warm laughter, and sudden tears when something got too much for her. Her strength after being assaulted by the drugged-up creep shouldn't have surprised him, but it had. Rosie had got to him in unexpected ways and yet he wasn't too worried. Which was a worry in itself because no, he absolutely shouldn't take a chance on finding love and happiness with her when he could end up hurting them both so badly.

'Go away, Rosie,' he muttered into his pillow. 'I need to sleep before we hit the road for Yarra Valley. Not to mention a room that we're sharing for two nights at the resort.'

* * *

The next thing Lucas was aware of was his phone making a racket beside the bed. He had the ring set on loud because he often slept through it after hectic nights on duty.

'Hello?'

'Did I wake you?' trilled Rosie.

'You've obviously been up for a while.' She sounded chirpy, even a little excited, which was hardly surprising considering she was going to her brother's wedding.

So am I.

Grand. He tossed the cover aside and hauled himself out of bed. 'What's the time?'

Laughter was her answer, followed by, 'Relax. It's barely gone two.'

'Two?' He never slept that late, even after a nightshift. 'What time am I picking you up?' It had taken some persuading for Rosie to accept he was driving She could be stubborn at times.

'We did agree on three, but let's change that to four. I've got a couple of things I need to do first.'

'Like give me time to have a strong coffee and a hot shower, by any chance?'

More laughter. 'You're onto it. Seriously, are you okay with four or thereabouts?'

'It works for me.'

He hadn't got around to packing what little

he was taking yet, but the new suit and shirt were hanging on the back of his bedroom door, and the shoes he'd bought to go with the suit were on the floor beneath, shining so much everyone would notice them. Might have to scuff them with just a little dirt... He grinned, suddenly feeling more relaxed about going away with Rosie. It had been easy to offer to be her date, but doubts had begun creeping in lately over whether he was doing the right thing for either of them. It could stretch their relationship beyond being friends, or it could kill it off totally if something went wrong.

Smile, man.

He was going away for the weekend and, while the circumstances were different, he *was* looking forward to time with Rosie. Even when she did screw with his head too much. Bring it on.

'Feel like stopping for a drink before we get to the resort?' Rosie looked at Lucas as they neared the valley. He looked good enough to enjoy in ways she hadn't done with any man for a while. 'I could do with some nibbles as I didn't have a lot for lunch.' Getting to know Lucas between the sheets would be even better.

Her face heated. Damn it. She was letting her guard down too far. It wasn't difficult around Lucas, but she had to stop. She couldn't afford to get intimate with him and then think they could carry on like they had for the last couple of weeks when they returned to the city. And that would be imperative. He wasn't stealing her heart, only for it to be broken later on when she withdrew.

'Sure thing. Do you know of somewhere to go?'

'No, but I'll have a look on my phone.' She hadn't been up this way in years. 'There are a few to choose from. Shall I keep it simple or do you want something fancy?'

'Leave fancy till tomorrow and the wedding.'

'Right. How about this one? It's a bar with outdoor dining and a view of the hills. The menu seems reasonable.'

Lucas flicked her a grin. 'Tell me where to go.'

That grin set off warning bells, reminding her she shouldn't be thinking about sex with Lucas, even when he grinned like that. It made him hot beyond description. This was not how the weekend was meant to play out and it was going to be hard sharing a room, and no doubt a bed, with him without stepping across the line from friends to something deeper. Not something more meaningful. She wasn't ready for that, and from what she'd seen, nor was Lucas. He didn't seem to have got over losing May yet.

'Take the next right.'

She was going to enjoy the stop, and then spending the evening with everyone before tomorrow's wedding. Was she going to enjoy spending time with Lucas? Absolutely. She was also going to be careful.

The bar wasn't too busy when they strolled in so they wouldn't be kept waiting for long, and for that her stomach was grateful.

'Can we sit outside?' she asked the young man behind the counter.

'Go for it. I'll bring menus out shortly. Would you like something to drink first?'

'Wine for me. One of the local Chardonnays, please. Lucas?'

'Make mine a beer, thanks, mate.'

Out under the canopy of trees, Lucas chose a table and held out a chair for her. 'Good choice.'

'Good advertising, more like it.' He was right though. The atmosphere was warm and friendly without being over the top, and the view was lovely. 'I feel like the weekend's started already.'

'It has. We don't have to be with everyone else for that to happen.' He sat opposite her and gazed around. 'I accept the circumstances are a little unconventional, but I'm looking forward to this, even though I don't know anyone else coming, and definitely not the bride and groom.'

Was he saying he wanted to spend more time with her? Well, despite that kiss and the thoughts it had raised, and the warnings going off in her head, so did she.

'Don't worry about not knowing anyone, because I don't know many of the people coming either. We'll stick together.'

'That'll fit in with the concept that we're a couple.'

The young man from the counter appeared with their drinks and menus. 'I'll give you a moment to decide what you'd like.'

'Don't rush,' Lucas told him, then lifted his glass and held it out to tap hers. 'Here's to a great weekend.'

It was as if he was being romantic. If she hadn't known why he was here in the first place she might've been hard pressed not to believe that.

'You surprised me when you offered to come, but I'm really grateful you did, and not just to shut my brother up. We get on well, and I'm glad we've reconnected. Let's make sure we don't lose touch again.'

'You're on. Now, tell me some things about Johnno so I don't make a complete fool of myself.'

'I'm going to let you suss him out for yourself.' Could be interesting to learn what Lucas thought about her brother by the end of the weekend. Johnno got very protective of her sometimes and could cross the line by being outspoken when it came to a man at her side. Which was why she struggled to understand why he'd been so persistent she hook up with Will.

Lucas shrugged. 'Fine. Why was he so intent on you being with his mate?'

'He wants me settled and happy. What he doesn't get is that I don't need him trying to set me up with his friends.'

'Especially Will.'

She nodded. 'Especially Will. I'm not incapable of meeting men and dating them as I see fit.' It sounded like Johnno thought she was hopeless, and she was far from it. She might have faults when it came to committing to a relationship but none when it came to finding great guys.

A glance at the one opposite made her draw a breath. She hadn't *found* Lucas, and he wasn't about to become her for ever partner, no matter how well they got on. It was a lot safer that way.

Lucas stared around the room Rosie had booked at the resort and pretended nothing was out of kilter. Hard to do with that huge, cosy bed taking up so much space. 'Tempting' was another word for it. How the hell was he going to stay on his side all night with Rosie lying so close he'd feel the heat coming off her? He wouldn't be able to sleep he'd be so rigid with keeping his hands to himself.

Not once when he'd offered to come along to save her from having to deal with Will had he thought sharing a bed would be so difficult. He wasn't meant to be thinking about her in any way other than someone he'd known years back and liked a lot. Certainly not as a woman who heated his blood and made his head spin with just a look. The woman who stirred him up fast. Since the night she'd been brought into the ED he'd been thrilled to see her and happy to go along with whatever either of them suggested doing outside of work but, so far, he had not wanted to bed her, to hold that sensational body in his arms and make love to her. Okay, that wasn't completely true because, more and more often, he'd been thinking about her in just that way, but nothing quite like the sensations gripping him now as he looked anywhere but at the beckoning bed.

'Not bad,' Rosie said as she hung her dress in the wardrobe. 'Give me your suit and I'll put it in here too.'

After handing his clothes to her, he stepped out onto the narrow balcony and leaned against the railing while he got his breathing under control. What the heck was going on? No way would he and Rosie have sex. They couldn't.

'Beautiful, isn't it?' Rosie stood beside him. 'So quiet too. The perfect place for a wedding.'

How had he missed her approaching? 'Shall we go down and catch up with everyone?' He needed to be busy, not standing around thinking about beds and sex.

'I guess we'd better or Johnno will be banging on the door demanding we join him.'

'Would he do that when he thinks we're a couple, staying in a romantic spot for the weekend?' Lucas closed his eyes for a moment. See what happened when he didn't think before he spoke? He'd just gone and put out there in a roundabout way what was going on in his head.

Rosie stared at him, surprise in her eyes. Then she nodded. 'You're right. He wouldn't. But still, let's go down and do the introductions.'

'Good idea.' He'd find a moment to talk to the concierge too. He'd come up with a way to put space between him and Rosie overnight.

'Hey, Rosie, there you are.' Downstairs, a tall, well-built guy wrapped his arms around her. 'Glad you made it.'

'As if I wouldn't.' She grinned. 'Johnno, this is Lucas Tanner.'

'Hey, Lucas, good to meet you.' The guy's handshake was firm, but the look he gave Lucas suggested he was going to make sure Lucas did right by his sister.

Locking his eyes on the man, Lucas returned the handshake just as firmly. 'Likewise, Johnno, and thanks for letting me accompany your sister to your wedding.'

'You're welcome. Not that I had a lot of choice who she brought.' His smile was cheeky, not annoyed, which made Lucas relax somewhat.

Lucas nodded. 'She knows her own mind, for sure.' She'd known exactly who she did not want to be partnered with for the weekend.

'How are the knocks and bruises?' Johnno asked Rosie.

'All but gone,' she replied.

Lucas studied her face and realised there wasn't any sign of the bruising that had coloured her chin and forehead after the assault. 'You're definitely looking a hundred percent back to normal.' Guess he hadn't taken a lot of notice because he'd been looking at the woman behind the smiles and tears and chatter. 'What can I get you to drink?' he asked her.

'Another wine would be lovely. Pinot Noir this time, if they have it.'

'You're in the Yarra Valley. Of course they have Pinot Noir,' Johnno cut in. 'This is red wine heaven.'

'I might try some too,' Lucas said. Not a huge wine drinker, he did enjoy most red varietals and if there was ever a time and place to indulge this was it.

'Johnno? Want one?'

'I'm good, thanks.' When Johnno followed him to the bar, he knew he was in for some questions. He just didn't know what about.

'I'm glad you were there for Rosie,' was the first thing Johnno said. 'She didn't say a lot about what happened when she was assaulted but I know she was freaking out that first day.'

'Agreed. She was, but she hid it well.'

'Give me time alone with the bastard who did that to her and he won't know what hit him.'

'You'll have to queue up behind me,' Lucas said firmly.

Johnno nodded. 'Thought I might have to.' He turned to the barman. 'Put this man's drinks on the tab, Harry. That goes for all night, along with my sister's.'

So he'd passed a test. There hadn't been any questions, but Johnno had been sussing him out in his own way.

'Thanks, Johnno. You didn't have to do that.'

'My night, my shout. Enjoy yourself.'

When Lucas returned to Rosie after a quick talk to the concierge with two glasses in hand, she took hers and nudged him lightly. 'I'll introduce you to everyone.'

There weren't many people here and they were all Johnno's friends.

'Karen's taken her lot to another restaurant for the evening. Some of the girls have been at the beauty spa this afternoon too,' Johnno told them.

Judging by her perfect pink nails, Rosie had done that back in the city at some point over the last couple of days. Lucas studied her face. 'You must be pleased with the way the bruising on your face has all but disappeared too.'

'Very pleased. I wasn't looking forward to being in the wedding photos looking like I'd been in a fight with a boxer and lost.'

'You never looked that bad,' he told her. Even when the puffy skin above her eye and on her chin was yellow, he'd thought she looked lovely. But then it seemed he was a bit off-centre when it came to Rosie these days.

'You're not good at telling porkies!' She laughed. 'But I'll take the compliment anyway. Can never get enough of them.'

There were plenty more where that one came from, but finally he'd got a grip on his mouth and was keeping it shut, except for enjoying the wine and looking around at the other guests grouped around a table at the far side of the room.

'Seems like there's a bit of a wine-tasting going on.'

Rosie looked in the same direction. 'It makes

sense considering we're at a vineyard, but it wasn't mentioned in the invitation.'

'They're probably making the most of having people here. Good way to sell cases of their product. Want to try some?'

'Not at the moment. I'm enjoying this Pinot Noir and don't really want to have another flavour mixing with it. Besides, I'm tired and want to be up to speed for tomorrow. Sorry if I'm being a wet blanket.'

He was quite relieved she wasn't interested because then he'd have had to join her and right now, he was more than comfortable with what was before him. The wine, that was.

'I'm happy sitting here taking my time with this glass.'

'We do think alike about some things, don't we?' Her smile was gentle and filled with happiness.

Because they got along so well? He hoped so.

'So last night's shift wore you out too? I admit working on Holly was draining. We were with her for what seemed like hours yet wasn't. Those burns were horrendous.' Some of the worst he'd ever seen. 'She was scheduled for plastic surgery this morning. Though only to deal with the worst sites. The plastic surgeon says she'll wait a few days before doing more work on the burns.'

Rosie shivered. 'Let's not go there tonight.'

'Fair enough.' Rosie was right to suggest he drop it. They were here for a wedding and to have some positive fun time, not focus on doom and gloom. 'What time did you knock off this morning?'

'Around seven. That call we got at the ED was for an elderly gentleman who'd had a stroke. I'm not sure why we were called and not the ambulance, but that's the way it goes sometimes.'

'Not your place to ask?'

'Not really, and anyway I'd rather be busy after the previous callout than sitting in the tearoom going over it all again and again.'

'Know what you mean.' So much for not talking about it. But he understood how sometimes it was nigh on impossible to let go the details of a case. 'I see they do a platter of breads and local cheeses here. Would you like one? I know we had a meal earlier but I wouldn't mind soaking up the wine with something light.'

That gentle smile returned. 'Like I said, we do think alike.'

It would be so easy to lean in and kiss her. Too easy. How would she react? Push him away or kiss him back? If she did, would the kiss be genuine or part of the ruse to keep Johnno off her back?

Lucas stood up and headed across to the guy behind the bar. 'Is it too late to order the cheese platter?' He had to ask, though he doubted it would be.

'Not at all. For two?'

'Please.'

Turning back to Rosie, he paused and drank in the sight of her. Even tired, she looked beautiful. His kiss would've been genuine. Right now, all he wanted to do was take her in his arms and hold her close, to savour her warm and caring nature, to take away the tension that had crept into her when talking about last night's patient. And kiss her. Again, he wondered if she'd appreciate it if he did. They were doing more than acting a role here this weekend, but the thing was, he'd discovered he wasn't really acting in any way. He was happy here with Rosie, and ready to go with the flow, wherever that led.

She turned and her eyes widened when she saw him watching her. 'Lucas?'

He joined her. 'It's all right. You haven't got a mess on your chin. I was thinking you look lovely in your pink blouse and cream trousers.' There, he could put it out there and not feel he'd made a mistake.

Her head tipped to the right and her smile widened. 'Thank you.' She blinked. 'I don't know what else to say.'

He laughed. So he wasn't in trouble. Not the get-out-of-my-face kind anyway. He might be thinking she was more than a friend, but he'd keep that to himself. He picked up his glass and took a long sip. It was a damned good Pinot Noir. 'I'm going to try some of the other reds while we're here. Might even buy a case or two to take back with us.' Us? 'We can enjoy them whenever we catch up.'

Rosie's laughter filled the air between them. 'I like that idea.' Then she leaned in and kissed his cheek, much like she'd been intending to that other time. Except tonight there were plenty of people around and he wasn't going to get too hot about wanting more, or show it anyway. Thank goodness he'd ordered a rollaway bed from the concierge or who knew how he'd have controlled himself sharing that super king size bed in their room. Offering to stand in as her partner for this wedding was turning out to be the craziest thing he'd done in a long time, yet he couldn't help loving every moment.

The platter appeared between them and the barman said, 'Here you go, folks. Enjoy.'

'Oh, we will,' Rosie told him, while still looking at Lucas.

Was she flirting with him? Lucas wondered. Surely not. But she had just kissed his cheek. Could he get that rollaway removed before she saw it? No, best not. He was getting ahead of himself. He did like Rosie a lot, even felt on the precipice of something more than just friendship, but he was rushing things. For himself and Rosie. They both needed to be careful going forward so neither would get hurt.

'Here, try this blue vein cheese.' She offered him a piece of bread with a wedge of the cheese on top.

He shook his head. 'No blue vein for me.' He picked up a knife and cut into the goat's cheese to spread on the softest bread he'd seen in a long while. 'This is more to my taste.'

'You don't know what you're missing out on,' Rosie said as she munched away.

As far as cheeses went, he certainly did. It was different when it came to Rosie, and tonight he was not going to find out. Tonight was all about playing safe. That decision was made, even if he came to regret it. They had a whole weekend to get through presenting as a happy couple to everyone, especially Johnno.

A big yawn rolled through Rosie like a tidal wave. Everything was catching up with her. Arduous night shifts, sleepless days due to reruns of being attacked beside her car, and trying to get past that kiss she and Lucas had shared last week. 'I think I'd better head to bed. I need to be in good form tomorrow.'

Lucas stared at his empty glass. 'I guess you do.'

Had mentioning the bed rocked him? It wasn't going to be easy sharing one. She was so aware of him in ways she shouldn't be that if he made a move on her, she knew she'd fall into his arms in a blink. She probably wouldn't even take that long.

'Would you like another wine?' She was done but she'd stay with him if he did. After all, he'd come here to make things easier for her.

He shook his head. 'No, I'm finished for the night as well.' He stood up and held his hand out to her. 'Come on. Let's go.'

Taking his hand, she stood up and looked around for Johnno. She found him watching them and tightened her grip on Lucas. They were meant to be a couple. A good excuse not to let Lucas go if ever there was one. His hand was firm around hers. Nice. More than nice. Hot, and filling her with a desperate longing she hadn't known in a long time, if ever. She should let go, but some things were impossible.

'Goodnight, Johnno. See you tomorrow.'

''Night, both of you.'

'Don't stay up all night,' she warned. 'You've got a big day ahead.'

'You're sounding like a mother, not sister.' Lucas grinned as he led her out of the room.

'Someone has to pretend to be keeping an eye on him.'

'He's being sensible. I haven't seen him drinking anything but water for the past hour or more.'

'That's my brother. And you're the one watching him, not me.' Laughter bubbled out of her. Lucas had just made her realise how seriously he was taking this weekend and being there for her. Not that she hadn't expected him to be totally involved but not to the point of watching out for Johnno, too.

He looked embarrassed. 'Sorry, that didn't come out how I meant it to. If Johnno's anything like I was the night before I got married, he'll be excited and nervous all in one and it's easy to get distracted by what everyone else is up to. Though, to be fair, everyone's been taking it easy with the wine.'

She nudged him. 'Including us.' She was trying to take in the fact he'd mentioned his wedding. That undercut her feelings of a moment ago and put her in her place.

'Rosie—' he turned to face her, an apologetic expression coming her way '—I shouldn't have mentioned my wedding. It's history and, despite what I told you, I have moved on enough to know I don't want it coming between us.'

'How can it? We're not a couple.'

His hand tightened around hers. 'Who knows what lies ahead?'

Pardon? She hadn't seen that coming. 'Not me, for certain.'

Her mind was a shambles when it came to what she really felt about Lucas. It was definitely more than friendship. Her reaction to him mentioning his wedding proved that. So did the happiness she'd known from the moment she'd got into his car to come up here. Lucas made her feel special, which gave her hope for the future. It was obvious in the way she reacted whenever she was close to him—like right now. Sparks flew whenever they touched. As for his kiss, it mightn't have got far but it had been sensational. Like a promise of more to come—a *good* more to come.

Being together seemed so right. It was an amazing feeling. A new feeling. Had she been wrong to accept his offer to come here? With these emerging feelings, it might be too easy to be swept away on a wave of passion and wake up to cold reality afterwards. Lucas hadn't got over losing May, something Rosie understood she couldn't compete with.

Lucas opened the door to their room and hesitated. 'Rosie, I asked for a rollaway bed to be brought to our room. I don't feel comfortable about sharing a bed with you, given we're only pretending to be a couple.'

Her heart sank at that reminder, but she conceded he was being sensible. Stepping past him, she swallowed at the sight of the made-up bed pushed against the far wall. Looking over her shoulder at him, she pulled on her big girl's pants. 'It's okay. I understand.'

I also feel unwanted.

Which she knew was totally unfair. She'd been hankering for some diversion with him, and had clearly deliberately misinterpreted things he'd said or done.

'I'm being a gentleman here.' His smile was tight.

She tried to be cheerful—hard to do when her heart was heavy. 'I'm not used to that.' Then she sighed. 'Come on. Let's move on. I am so glad to have you here with me that you don't need to keep apologising for everything you do.'

If only he wasn't being cautious about their original agreement. But then if he wasn't she'd probably find fault with that too. She wasn't easy to please. Yet she felt so different about Lucas, so relaxed whenever she was with him. Was this because she'd already known him as a friend? Knew that when he'd given his heart to May it was for ever? Did that make it easier to give in to the other emotions swamping her when she was with him, unlike other men she'd spent time with? Because she felt safe to do so as he didn't return her feelings?

Right now, she had no answers. Instead of overthinking it she was going to bed. Tomorrow would be a big day. Her brother had found the love of his life, which suggested it might be possible for her too. If so, bring it on.

Sliding under the bedcover, she admitted she might be getting nearer to opening up to love. This new sense of wanting to let go and give love a chance was scary—and exciting. Because of Lucas? Was he the cause? Was it him she was willing to share her heart with? No definite answer came, instead more of a softening in her chest and a warmth settling over her. Lucas was special, either way.

CHAPTER SIX

'HERE, USE THIS.' Lucas handed Rosie a perfectly folded handkerchief from his jacket pocket.

This man was perfect. Who had handkerchiefs these days? Rosie sniffed and wiped her cheeks, where tears were slowly tracking through her make-up. Leaning close to Lucas, she said quietly as she watched Johnno walk down the aisle with a beaming Karen on his arm, 'I am so happy for him. He deserves this day.' They were sitting with all the guests in the beautifully appointed room with a glass wall overlooking the vineyards where the marriage celebrant had just pronounced Johnno and Karen married.

Lucas took her free hand and held it lightly on his thigh. 'Everyone does.'

Except the creep who'd assaulted her. She blinked. Where had that come from when she was full of such happy emotions? Could be that emotion was getting to her in more ways than she needed.

'You're right. They do.' Lucas did. She did.

She'd go for that and forget the one who didn't. He didn't belong here—not today or any other day.

As everyone stood up to follow the bride and groom through to the massive outside deck, Lucas wound an arm around Rosie's waist and tucked her in against his side. 'Come on. Let's celebrate this special occasion.'

'You say that when you barely know the bride and groom.'

'I know, but there's something wonderful about a truly happy wedding—and, before you say it, there are some that are nowhere close to happy. Believe me, I went to one once and wanted to shout at the couple to see sense and go their separate ways. The angst was coming off them in waves. Turned out they were marrying because she was pregnant and he refused to let her have the baby unwed. Some history there that I knew nothing about, and still don't.'

'Where did you fit into the picture?'

'He worked at the same hospital as me in San Fran and I don't think he had a lot of friends. Most of the guests on his side were from the hospital and didn't know him well.'

'I'd rather get married with no one there to celebrate if that was the case.'

'I'll come.'

'Got to find a man to marry, yet.' Did Lucas

have an answer for that? Judging by the silence that followed, he didn't. 'Actually, I haven't been looking.'

They'd reached the garden setting, where waiters were handing around glasses of champagne. Lucas took two and passed her one. 'Why not?'

'Think I've already said I struggle with risking my heart.'

'You did mention that but, to my way of thinking, if you don't give it a go, you'll never know if you can move past your fears.'

Her eyebrows rose as she stared at him. 'Really?'

'Yes, okay, I should know better than to put myself on the mat like that. But seriously, Rosie, do you truly want to remain single and miss out on what you could have for the rest of your life?'

'No, I don't.'

'I rest my case.' He gave her a gentle, almost loving, smile.

'Do you?'

His smile disappeared. 'Not really. But I have some things to get over first.'

She winced. She'd known that. 'Sorry, I should've kept quiet.'

His smile returned slowly, and it was genuine. 'It's fine.' He sipped his champagne. 'Let's drop serious and go with fun. Enjoy the moments.'

Lucas made everything seem so plausible, and

so easy to do. She'd give it a crack and see how the day unfolded, because she couldn't think of anyone else she'd rather be here celebrating her brother's day with than Lucas.

'Hello, Rosie.' Will appeared in front of them.

She straightened a little more, and smiled when Lucas drew her closer. 'Hello, Will. How are you?'

'Fine, thank you.'

'Will, this is Lucas Tanner, my partner.' Weren't her pants supposed to catch fire when she lied? But it wasn't a lie, she reminded herself. Lucas was partnering her for the weekend. How Will interpreted 'partner' was his to decide.

'Hello, Will.' Lucas held his hand out to the guy.

Will ignored him. 'It's good to see you, Rosie. I'll talk to you later.' With that, he turned and strode away.

'Plonker,' she muttered.

'So that's the wonderful Will.' Lucas looked to her. 'Even if I say so, you can do much better than that, Rosie.'

She laughed. 'I already am.' Then she shivered. 'He really has an ego that needs trimming down to size.' Why Johnno thought she'd fall for Will she couldn't imagine.

She thought that again when she went to chat with Karen's mother. Will was standing to the side, watching her as though he owned her. *Creepy* came to mind. But was she being too harsh? He might have trust issues too. Still, not her problem when he'd been so rude to her the one time they had dated.

'Rosie, got a minute?' Will asked when she left Karen's mother to go back to Lucas, who seemed happy chatting with some of Johnno's mates.

Not really, but she didn't want to cause a scene or be rude. 'Sure.'

'Are you serious about that guy you came with? He's not worthy of you.'

'Will, you don't even know Lucas.' Her blood began to simmer. 'He's very much an honourable man, more than worthy of me.'

'Aww, come on. You'd be way better off with me.'

'Which bit of "I am not interested" don't you get, Will?'

'Open your eyes, Rosie. You have no idea what you're turning down. I can give you everything you want and more. I'm wealthy and an outstanding lawyer to boot.'

'You're an idiot, is what you are,' Lucas said from beside Rosie.

Thank you, Lucas.

She turned away from the arrogant man trying to loom over her and took Lucas's hand to pull him away. She didn't look back, instead moved closer to her saviour. 'Let's find somewhere more conducive to a great time.'

'How about a walk in the vineyard?'

The sun was low in the sky and the temperature balmy. Other people were already making the most of the open space and waiters were out there, refilling glasses as they wandered around.

'Let's.'

'I can't believe that man,' Lucas ground out. 'Who does he think he is?'

'William John Clark the first.' She giggled, back to happy mode. It took no time at all with Lucas at her side.

'The first? I feel for the poor little blighter that follows in the family line.' Lucas was grinning too.

'We're here to enjoy the night.'

Lucas leaned closer. 'The night is but barely started.'

Rosie sighed. He was quite something. Special didn't begin to describe him. How had she not noticed this when she'd known him before? More than likely because she'd been with Cameron and relatively happy. Just nothing like this. Anyway, Lucas had been married to May then. She didn't check out married men. Now it was obvious how considerate and kind and loving Lucas was. Loving as in being there for others, not so much as in handing her his heart on a plate. He and May had seemed the perfect couple after all, and she doubted she'd ever come up to May's standard. From the little he'd said about May and what had happened, she doubted he'd be ready for a deep and meaningful relationship for a while to come. But there also seemed to be more to his story than he was prepared to share and until he did she couldn't fully trust him. But he could be up for something hot and sexy. Like she suddenly was.

Drawing a deep breath, she went for caution. She didn't want to scare him off. As he'd said, the night was young. 'Where's a wine waiter when I need one?' When had she finished her champagne? Might be wise to slow down. But then, wise could be overdone at times and tonight was special because it was about her family. A very small family, but it had just grown with Karen and her lot becoming part of Johnno's life and therefore, in a small way, hers too.

Lucas looked around. 'Over there.' He took her hand and led her across to the young woman standing with a laden tray in hand.

They wandered along the rows of vines, still holding hands and saying little. It was a companionable silence, something Rosie wasn't used to. She felt as though this was another step in getting to know each other better. They didn't have to fill in the silence with idle chitchat all the time, and could be themselves without worrying what the other was thinking. Yes, she was usually like that with the men she'd dated, always wondering what was coming next, and if she wanted to continue being with them. If they liked her enough to stay with her and not walk out of her life just when she'd become vulnerable to them. She didn't think that with Lucas—but then they weren't in a relationship, she reminded herself.

'Excuse me, but everyone is requested to make their way to the dining room now.' A waitress had appeared in front of them. 'The celebrations are about to begin.'

'We're on our way.' Lucas grinned as they headed for the building. 'There's something special about seeing a couple sharing their most important moments, even when I don't know them.' He flicked her a brief glance, looked away again.

Her breath stopped in the middle of her chest. Wow. She squeezed his hand. 'I know what you mean.' She really did, though until now she'd never believed she might one day have those special moments herself. Since meeting up with Lucas again, all sorts of notions regarding love and permanency were taking over her mind and making her consider the possibility of letting herself be vulnerable. But then she'd immediately return to why she held herself back and bury the hope that had flared.

'Would you like a nightcap?' Lucas asked Rosie as they walked through their room to the small deck overlooking the winery. 'There's wine in the fridge or we can order something else if you'd prefer.'

'Wine's fine. A small one. I've already had more than I usually do.'

What the heck? She was having a good time with Lucas, the most wonderful man she'd known. He'd been there for her all day, had shared the fun and laughter with a complete group of strangers. And he was so handsome her mouth watered looking at him.

'You're doing fine.' His smile touched her deeply. 'How does it feel to see your brother so happy?'

'I'm thrilled. He already seems so much happier than last time. I think Karen's more his type and will be there for ever. Fingers crossed,' she added quietly.

'I'll drink to that.'

Out on the deck, Lucas leaned against the railing. Rosie joined him, letting her shoulder touch his lightly, hoping he wouldn't move away. He didn't, instead leaned in closer, his shoulder pressing against hers, his hip touching her side. Did he want more too?

Rosie took a big gulp and turned to put her glass down on the tiny table. To hell with this. Sometimes a person had to take risks, chance their feelings. It felt as if this was her moment.

Turning back to Lucas, she leaned in to kiss him, as in slide her tongue into his mouth and press her lips firmly against his like she had no intention of backing off any time soon. Her hands slid around his waist and tugged him against her love-starved body, which tightened in an instant. Still holding his wine, he hauled her in against him even more closely.

It was so good. Better than good. Amazing to feel him up against her. He was returning her feverish kiss, touch for touch, taste for taste. Then he was kneading her bottom and she was beyond thinking.

Except for, 'Bed?' Then she continued kissing him.

He must've put his glass down at some point because when he laid her on the bed both his arms were holding her firmly against that wide, deliciously muscular chest of his. She didn't let him go as she sprawled over the bed, instead held him tightly so he had to follow her. As if he wouldn't. They'd started something they couldn't stop. Winding her legs around him, she trailed kisses over his chin, neck, down to his chest, tasting him, feeling his hard length pressing into her.

A fierce need filled Lucas. Rosie was above him, unbuttoning his shirt as she kissed his chest, then his nipples, sending desire sparking throughout his hungry body.

He reached for her dress, tried to lift it over her head.

She stopped kissing his overheated skin long enough to wriggle her way out of the figure-hugging dress and reveal a low-cut lacy bra and minimal matching lace panties that accentuated her stunning body. Then she went back to running those hot lips all over his body. Chest, stomach and lower, even lower, till he had to stop her or this would be over before they'd really got started.

Wrapping his arms around her, he reversed their positions, flipping Rosie beneath him. Holding her hands above her head, he began to return the favour—kissing first one beautiful full breast then the other until she shivered and cried out. He worked his way down to her navel and beyond, feeling her body getting tighter all the way.

'Lucas,' she groaned as her hips bucked up against him. 'Lucas, stop. I can't take any more.'

Oh, yes, you can, and you will.

The words never left his mouth. He was too busy showing her.

Then her body tensed, and jerked upward. 'Lucas, join me. Now.'

'One moment.' Grabbing his trousers, he found the condom he'd placed there earlier just in case. All right, he finally admitted he'd been hoping they'd get together in bed. His need had been growing ever since they'd arrived at the resort.

'Lucas…' Those luscious lips encased his nipple, sent fire through his veins.

Then he was sliding inside her, feeling her heat engulf him, and he was lost in sensation.

Coming to some time later, he wrapped Rosie in his arms and rolled onto his back, keeping her close. A smile spread across his face. Rosie could lose control after all, and he'd seen it up close. What a different woman she was when she did. He'd like to see a lot more of that in all aspects of her life.

As she sprawled across him, she hauled her eyes open and grinned at him. 'Wow. I am so glad you came with me.'

He chuckled. 'That could be taken two ways.'

'Both ways count.' Her breath was hot on his skin.

He held her tighter. No way was he letting

her go any time soon. Never had he been with a woman and felt so relaxed and yet wired all at once. This was something else. He'd offered to accompany her to this wedding as she'd needed a date and here they were, recovering from the most intense sexual encounter he'd experienced in years. Another step forward. More like a leap. Whichever, he felt good and so at ease it was incredible.

He whispered, 'Thank you, Rosie.'

Lifting her head, she kissed him lightly. 'Back at you.' Then she curled up beside him and wound an arm around his waist and closed her eyes.

Lucas continued holding her warm body against his as she slipped into sleep. Through the wide glass doors, he watched the stars twinkling above the vineyard. A perfect ending to a wonderful day. He couldn't wish for anything more.

But when Rosie woke an hour later and turned to touch him, he knew he was beyond ready for more. Far more. The scary thing being he didn't want it to ever end.

Rosie woke slowly, snuggled in against Lucas with his arm over her waist.

Wow. What a night. She couldn't remember ever feeling quite so relaxed and happy after an intimate night as she did now. There was something so easy about being with Lucas that had her feeling comfortable and not looking for trouble. He was trustworthy, which meant a lot, but she still wasn't looking for anything long-term with him. They remained friends, which was more important as there was less chance of that going wrong. Yet, after the night she'd just experienced, she had to admit to wanting to open up and let him in a little more than usual. Apart from her dad when she was very young, there hadn't been another man she'd ever felt so trusting with. Yeah, and look how her father had let her down. If he couldn't love her, then who could she trust to do so?

'Morning, sunshine. You look rather troubled.' Lucas was watching her carefully.

To get serious or relax and have some more fun? The answer was simple.

'Hello, you. I was worrying you wouldn't wake up early enough to make love again before we get ready to go to the family breakfast.' The two families were getting together this morning for a meal before the newlyweds headed to the airport to fly out to Hobart for their honeymoon.

'All you had to do was kiss me and I'd have woken instantly.' Lucas grinned and reached for her, tugging her over him, already erect.

She could get used to this, she thought as she slid down and covered him. Very much so.

* * *

They were late to breakfast but no one seemed to care. Everyone was in a cheerful mood and there was lots of laughter going around the table as Lucas held out a chair for Rosie.

'You two look happy,' Johnno called from the other end with a cheeky big brother glint in his eyes.

'Thanks for sharing that,' Rosie muttered under her breath. She might have opened up to Lucas but she wasn't into sharing her hot night with others, especially people she didn't know well. 'I think you and Karen take the award for that.' She could give as good as she got. To be fair, Johnno looked the happiest she could ever recall.

'Would you like a glass of bubbles?' Karen's father, Bill, asked her. 'We're making the most of breakfast before everyone heads off to their normal lives, except for these two, of course.' He nodded at his daughter and Johnno.

'I'd love one,' Rosie said before downing a glass of water.

'Lucas?' Bill waved the bottle at him.

'Why not?' Lucas held out a glass, then tapped it against hers. 'Cheers.'

'Cheers.' She took a small sip before picking up the menu. 'I'm starving.' Laughter broke out around the table and she could feel her cheeks heating. 'What?'

'You're not the first to say that this morning,' someone called out.

Glancing at her brother and his wife, Rosie immediately knew who he was referring to. This was getting a bit much. She hadn't been on her wedding night. It had been a wonderful experience but she and Lucas weren't exactly tying the knot any time soon. Turning to Lucas, she gulped. He looked as if he was about to burst into laughter and probably say something to make her even more embarrassed.

'What are you having for breakfast?' she asked in a hurry.

He leaned close and said quietly, 'I've had my first course.'

The heat in her face deepened and she looked away. This was getting awkward.

'Have you all put your orders in?' she finally managed.

'We were waiting for you,' Bill told her. 'Want some coffee while you make up your mind?' He looked sympathetic in an amused kind of way. 'Lucas?'

'Definitely.' Totally at ease, Lucas handed over their cups to the waiter. Obviously, none of this was getting to him. 'Thanks, mate.'

'If I ever get married, I am not having the

morning-after breakfast,' Rosie decided. There again, if she ever did take the chance and tied the knot, why not have everyone there to share her happiness with? Taking a big gulp of coffee, she studied the menu, more for a distraction than to decide what to eat because she always had Eggs Benedict when out for breakfast.

'Eggs Benedict for me,' Lucas told her.

She grinned. 'Once more, we're on the same page.'

Even after an eventful night, he still looked marvellous. Knowing that sexy body better made it harder to hold onto her caution. Funny how they'd started out as friends and were now lovers. A boundary had definitely been crossed but for some reason she wasn't worried about it. Not a lot, anyway. Where they went from here was anyone's guess. Right now, she'd make the most of having Lucas with her. Sliding her hand under the table, she squeezed his thigh lightly. Touching him felt good, brought up thoughts of everything that had happened last night.

Lucas covered her hand with his and squeezed back. 'Happy?' he asked quietly.

'Absolutely.' She really was. 'You?'

'What do you think?' He grinned.

She laughed. 'Same page?'

He nodded. 'This is getting to be quite a story, isn't it?'

'I think so.'

Were they rushing things? She hoped not. Last night had been the perfect ending to a wonderful day. Lucas coming to the wedding with her had been a natural offer on his behalf. That they'd picked up their friendship when they'd caught up again had been a no-brainer. No rushing was going on. It was all a natural progression. Towards what? The answer would surely come later. Right now, she wasn't getting tied up in second-guessing herself. She was going to keep making the most of what she had.

When breakfast was over and everyone was leaving the table, Johnno came over and pulled her into a big hug. 'I like Lucas,' he told her quietly. 'You're different with him in a good way.'

'He's special, no doubt about it.' She could admit that to her brother because he'd keep it to himself. She wouldn't point out it was him who'd been insisting she hook up with his mate. 'Have a great time in Hobart.'

Johnno pulled back. 'We will, I promise.' He stepped across to Lucas and shook his hand. 'I'm glad you came with Rosie to our wedding.'

Lucas's eyes widened a little but he returned the handshake comfortably enough. 'So am I, Johnno. All the best for everything.'

'You, too.'

Rosie's heart melted a little as she watched the

men. They were getting along fine, which made her happy as long as Johnno wasn't reading too much into the fact Lucas had spent the weekend with her. It had been wonderful but where to from here was anyone's guess. Yep, she was suddenly coming down off the high last night had brought on.

Lucas was an awesome man, but that whole trust thing was raising its ugly head again. How could she believe he'd stay for ever if they got into a serious relationship? The truth was, she couldn't. Couldn't trust anyone to love her for ever, not even Lucas. It wasn't in her DNA.

So she'd make the most of the remainder of the weekend and then get back to business. Friends only. Maybe friends with benefits, if that suited Lucas too. Because it was impossible to deny they'd hit it off so well in bed. Until now, she hadn't known sex could be so effortless and mind-blowing. As a lover Lucas was out of this world.

'Want to come up?' Rosie asked as Lucas parked outside her apartment building that afternoon.

He shouldn't. They couldn't carry on as if they were a real couple. Not when he still had difficulty believing he wouldn't hurt her along the way. Nor when he was still protecting his heart.

'You bet.' His tongue had a way of taking over

from his mind at times, and he had to admit he wasn't unhappy with its answer to Rosie's offer. Of course she could be going to make him coffee and nothing else, but he already knew what that wicked gleam in her eyes meant and coffee had nothing to do with it. And if he was in the tiniest bit of doubt the sexy smile she gave him reiterated that. The same smile that he'd seen often throughout the night had relentlessly amped up his desire for her.

Locking his car after getting her bag out of the boot, he did remind himself he had to be careful. He was guilty in part for May's accident. It could happen in another way all too easily and he did not want to lose the next woman he settled down with.

In her apartment, Rosie led the way to her bedroom, not even stopping to put her bag down.

Lucas had to laugh as anticipation worked its way through him, tightening him everywhere, heating his skin and raising his pulse. Whatever happened, they were going to have some fun now. Fun he would not regret, no matter what else went down. Rosie had got to him, and he enjoyed being with her. He wouldn't look too far ahead at the moment. Time to think about his needs, to enjoy making love with Rosie since she was more than willing to join him in this madness, however temporarily.

Without a word to disrupt the mood, they were under the covers and reaching for each other in unison. They already knew each other well and it could only get better. Couldn't it?

'Rosie, wait, let me touch you first.'

Later, when they sat up and leaned back against the pillows, Lucas's face was warm and his body languid. 'I haven't made out so often in such a short time since I don't know when.'

Rosie's eyes widened. 'I'm not sure if that's a compliment or an insult, being reminded you've had other lovers while we're in bed.'

He'd blown it. Now she'd send him to purgatory. Grabbing her hand, he held her lightly. 'I'm sorry, Rosie. That came out all wrong. I wasn't thinking about anyone else, I assure you. I've had a wonderful time and got carried away with it all. Plus, I'm feeling happier than I have for ages.'

'So it was a compliment?' Was she feeling uncared about?

'Absolutely. I thought you were wonderful before we went to the Yarra Valley and now I know so.' He stopped. What did he want to say? How to say it?

'I'm listening.'

What if he just shoved the past away and got on with enjoying a future with Rosie? If she wanted one with him. Taking her face in his hands, he locked eyes with her. 'Rosie, I'd love to spend more time with you. Maybe have a fling and see how we get along on a deeper level, if you're up for that?'

Her eyes widened, then blinked. A red hue coloured her face. Was that a yes or a get lost look? He held his breath, paralysed by how much he longed for her to say yes.

'Lucas, I—' She was going to tell him to go leap off her balcony and not come back. 'Lucas, I'd like to do that very much.'

Relief poured through him, quickly followed by excitement. 'No promises about the future.' He had to put it out there, just in case she read too much into his suggestion.

'Once more, we're on the same page.' She leaned in to kiss his cheek, then his mouth, as if she was sealing a deal.

He had no problem with that. Holding her tight, he knew he couldn't have let her go completely, maybe not at all.

One step at a time.

CHAPTER SEVEN

'MULTI-CAR PILE-UP on a suburban street. Teens doing wheelies,' Rosie told Lucas and Connor, a nurse, when they had landed at the hospital next Friday night. 'Three seriously injured. Your patient appears to be in her teens. She's unconscious and has been all the time we've been with her. Skull injury on the right. Because of that we're treating this as a spinal injury and have placed a neck brace on her.'

'Makes sense.'

Rosie nodded, and continued filling him in. 'She didn't react to my touch on her feet or legs. I did get slight movement when I felt her arms and chest.'

He nodded, still checking the girl for himself. Nothing unusual there.

'There's severe bleeding from her right wrist, which also has multiple fractures. Right hip and thigh appear to have taken some impact also.'

'No idea who she is?' Lucas asked as he took one corner of the trolley.

'None. The police are onto it but it could be a while before you know anything as all the passengers in the same car were unconscious.' She glanced sideways at Lucas, who flicked her a brief smile before returning his focus to the girl.

'It must've been one hell of a crash.'

'The car was unrecognisable. Alcohol's suspected, and possibly drugs.'

'Not uncommon,' Lucas commented. 'Right now, that's only one of our worries. We'll check for both once we've stabilised her.'

They were inside and heading towards the lift, everyone crowded around the trolley monitoring the girl's monitors and reactions. It wasn't looking good.

'Heart rate's dropping,' Connor warned.

'Get ready to perform CPR,' Lucas said while pushing the trolley inside the lift.

Rosie pressed the button for the floor the emergency department was on, all the while watching the girl and the heart monitor. Suddenly, 'Flatline.'

Connor was already onto it with the ECG attached to the girl's chest. 'Stand back.'

One charge and the line was moving up and down again. 'Phew,' Rosie said aloud.

'Too right,' Lucas agreed as he studied the monitor.

The lift slowed, stopped, and they were rolling

the trolley into the ED, where they had to shift their patient from the spinal board onto the bed without any movement to her body. As soon as they were done, Rosie picked up the board. She needed to get back to the chopper. 'Right, I'm on my way. Got another patient from the same accident to collect.'

Lucas barely nodded, focused on the girl.

She leaned closer, said quietly, 'See you later.'

He nodded without looking round. 'Yes.'

'Where are we taking our next patient?' she asked the pilot once on board the chopper.

'Same hospital. Everyone's crazy busy to-night.'

'Of course they are. It's the beginning of the weekend.'

Always the worst night to be on the roster. So many people out on the town having a blast, getting tanked and then driving or brawling. Which would be why they were picking up the next patient, who wasn't in such a bad way as the last one. Every available ambulance would be out and about around the city. It was never nice dealing with the worst cases as there was often someone lurking in the background de-manding attention and looking for more trou-ble. Thankfully, that hadn't been the case when they'd picked up the girl they'd just delivered to Lucas's emergency department.

Lucas. She hadn't once bumped into him at his work until she'd been taken there as a patient. The flights she worked on didn't often go to Parkville as the hospital was close to the CBD and the patients Rosie dealt with were more often from the outskirts of the city or rural areas. Yet now she seemed to be going to Parkville quite often. Life had a way of throwing curve balls, but in her case they weren't always bad ones. She loved seeing Lucas in the department and working on patients alongside him.

He'd definitely got to her. Something she had not expected. His lovemaking was beyond wonderful, but that wasn't her reason for starting to let go and fall for him. It was more to do with the way he'd supported her after she'd been assaulted, how he'd gone to the wedding with her, the way he treated her as an equal, as someone special, that rattled her and had her wondering if she could take a chance on having more with him than only a fling. As in letting in the love she felt for him. But it was scary. So much could go wrong.

'Here we go. You ready back there?' asked the pilot.

Rosie glanced at Dave, the paramedic on this shift with her, who gave her a grin. 'When aren't we?'

'That's a yes,' she told the pilot. Dave was a

bit of a hard case, she'd discovered. He was new to the team but very experienced after working for Rescue Flights in Sydney. 'You take the lead on this one.' It was his turn.

'Cheers, Rosie. I'll try not to make a mess of things.' That grin was ongoing.

'Hope not.' She laughed and looked out of the window as the ground came up to meet them. The scene hadn't changed a lot from when they'd lifted away before with the unconscious young woman. There were more police, but the crowd was still there.

'Jane Duncan, nineteen, probably fractured ankle and tibia.' The paramedic attending the woman stood up as they approached. 'She was lucid but has gone into shock. Admitted to drinking a lot.'

'We'll take over now,' Dave said. 'How come you're still here? I thought all ambulances were tied up with other cases.'

'They are. My lot are two streets away, dealing with a minor case at a house. I'll go meet up with them now.' He looked around. 'One of the cops is giving me a lift.'

Rosie wasn't surprised. The emergency services crews helped each other in these situations. She watched Dave as he checked on Jane. 'Ready to load up?' Sounded like she was referring to a slab of cargo. 'Jane, we're going to put you on a trolley and take you across to the helicopter. Is that all right?'

'Whatever.'

Dave gave Rosie a shrug and she reciprocated. They'd get on with the job and keep the conversation with Jane to a minimum.

When they rolled Jane into the emergency department Lucas was at a desk entering notes into the computer and looked up when she said, 'Back again. This time it's not urgent.'

'I'll be with you in a moment.' Then he winked. 'Catch up after work? Do some more… de-stressing?'

'Perfect.' Sex at her apartment, eat, get some sleep. Together. Sounded ideal.

'Sure, no problem,' Lucas answered the department head's plea for help the next morning. 'I'll be there as soon as possible.' The early day shift was down a doctor and a nurse who lived together due to a stomach bug apparently doing the rounds. Another doctor was coming in later in the morning so Lucas was going straight back in to carry on until then.

So much for putting a second coat of paint on the lounge walls. But going into work would keep his mind busy and less focused on thinking about Rosie and how much he was enjoying her company. It was hard to think of her as only a friend with benefits. Too hard. He grunted. Hard being a word he shouldn't use when thinking about Rosie. It described exactly what happened whenever he did.

The sex was amazing, and there'd be more to come. But that was only the beginning. Whenever he was with her, whether sitting over a drink or travelling to Yarra or chatting on the phone, he felt so relaxed and unencumbered with guilt, or even his fear of being hurt again. He felt alive. Like he used to feel before May died.

He hadn't always been on top of the world then, but he'd been largely happy with his life and where it was headed—until May had told him about moving to Sydney. Perhaps they hadn't been perfectly matched after all. Or they'd grown apart as they got older and found they wanted different things for their futures.

He shook his head in shock. Until now, he'd refused to really admit that to himself. When she'd told him she was moving to Sydney regardless of what he wanted and was furious at his need to discuss it, he'd been angry too. Naturally, she'd been excited about her promotion and his negative response to moving without at least talking about it must've been like having a wet blanket thrown over her. But she hadn't once paused to think about his side of things, had been so determined to take up the offer that he didn't feature in the decision. That had hurt big time.

But, looking back, he knew there'd been other incidents in the months leading up to that night where May had commented about him choosing emergency medicine instead of becoming a GP and setting up his own practice, something he'd always said he didn't want. She'd started focusing on making more money instead of what they'd agreed to do. Then she'd decided that having a family would harm their careers. That had gutted him more than the rest of her complaints. The cracks had been there in their marriage all along. He'd just denied the existence of them.

Was he remembering it all now because of Rosie? Yes, he was. Rosie was becoming more important to him every day. Even the days when he didn't see her, he couldn't stop thinking about her. This had nothing to do with a convenient and friendly fling. It was about having the whole deal. A deal he still wasn't ready to get tied into. He could still hurt Rosie. He could still stuff this all up.

Except how much of what had happened to May that night really was his fault? She'd completely lost her temper and, by all accounts, driven like a racing driver through the city. He wasn't denying he'd argued with her, but it hadn't been his decision for May to get behind the steering wheel.

Lucas spun around on his heel, looking at the room he stood in. Where was this coming from? He'd always taken more than his share of the blame so why was he changing his mind now? The answer was as clear as a summer sky. He wanted to live life fully, not half-heartedly. It seemed that might be possible with Rosie. If he was brave enough to risk it.

But right now, he needed to get a move on. Grabbing his keys, he headed out of the door. No more thinking about the woman driving him mad with desire. He had a job to do and each patient needed his full attention, and he was more than happy to oblige.

Less than an hour later, when he was sitting at the desk filling in some notes on a toddler who'd fallen out of her cot and got a black eye, the phone interrupted him. 'Emergency department, Lucas speaking.'

'Emergency response. We've got a chopper on the way to you with a male victim of a stabbing to the chest. Code purple. ETA ten minutes.'

'On my way up to the top.' He dropped the phone. 'Jason and Coop, code purple on the roof.' He didn't say any more. They knew what to do. Instead, he thought of all the symptoms the patient could be, and probably was, suffering. A stab to the chest endangered the lungs or the heart—or, worst case scenario, both. Heart failure was high on the list, as was compromised breathing. Who was the doctor on board? Because this person was going to need the absolute best there was.

The victim was getting it, Lucas noted the moment the chopper door opened. Rosie hadn't signed off yet. She was right beside the trolley being pushed by Dave, with her hands pressed into the patient's groin. There was blood everywhere.

'I thought the serious wound was in the chest,' Lucas said when he reached them.

'Yep, that too,' Rosie muttered. 'We haven't got a tally of how many wounds there are.' She was fully focused on dealing with the massive blood loss going on under her hand.

Dave was frantically keeping an eye on all the monitors while pushing the trolley towards the door.

Lucas grabbed a corner of the trolley. 'I'll take this. You keep on doing what else you're focused on.'

'Get us downstairs ASAP.' Rosie flicked him a look of desperation. 'I daren't shift my hands at all.'

The nurse who'd come up with Lucas had the

lift door open and took the other end of the trolley to guide it inside.

'As soon as we get down, Jason, go sort out the suturing. This can't wait.' Lucas hadn't taken his eyes off Rosie and the wound she was trying to keep from completely bleeding out. The tension in her face told him how worried she was that the man wouldn't make it. 'The femoral vein?' he asked, though already guessed it was. He just wanted to hear her voice.

She nodded abruptly. 'I've been pressing on it for twenty minutes or more, but I don't have an accurate time for when the injury happened. The police didn't know either.'

'What about the chest injury?'

'His breathing's shallow but no sign of a pierced lung, though I've been a bit distracted.' She gave him a tight smile.

'Dave?'

'It seems the knife went downward rather than directly into the lung cavity.'

'Could've been deflected by the ribs.' The lift stopped. 'Right, let's move fast.' He didn't have to add 'carefully'. Everyone knew what was required. He'd really been talking for the sake of it. 'Jason, get onto the blood bank too. We're going to need two litres to start with.'

'Onto it.'

'Thank goodness you're here,' Rosie said. 'It's good having you here to work with on this.'

He felt a moment of pride at her words. 'How long have you got?'

'As long as it takes. The pilot's going to wait unless there's another call.'

Under the lights that lit up the bed, Lucas studied the injury site that was visible around Rosie's fists. 'This is going to be tricky.'

Jason already had the suture kit beside the man with everything laid out exactly as needed. Another nurse was attaching monitors to the exposed chest to replace the rescue helicopter's equipment.

Lucas threaded a suture needle. 'Dave, be ready to dab away any seepage the moment Rosie moves her hands.'

'Right.'

'Ready, everyone.' He held the needle close to the severed vein, where Dave had a swab. 'Rosie, take away the pressure.'

Instantly, the wound was apparent. Lucas slid the needle into the vein and pulled the edges together and tied off the first stitch. Then the next one and the next one. Another nurse had another needle threaded for the moment he ran out of thread. Once he'd done that he began on the outer wound. It seemed to take for ever to finish. Thankfully, the bleeding had slowed, making the job easier, but it was also bad news for the patient as it meant his blood level had dropped too far.

'Here's the first two litres of blood,' Jason said, already setting up the stand with the bag.

'Rosie, would you mind checking it?' He was too busy sewing and Rosie wasn't required to press on the wound any longer.

'Onto it.' Moments later, she said, 'I'm looking at the chest wound now.'

'What are you finding?'

'There was evidence of quite a lot of bleeding when we first got to the man, but it's stopped now.' Her fingers were moving over the ribs, starting with the side where the knife had gone in. If it had been a knife.

'Do we know for sure what the weapon was?'

'The cops found a knife in the bushes beside where this man lay. But no guarantees that was it,' she added. 'They'll send it to forensics. In the meantime, they're still searching the area for another likely weapon.'

He glanced at the heart monitor. 'Heart-rate's dropped.'

'I'm not taking my eyes off the screen,' one of the nurses told him. She had the defib attached to the man and she was ready to press the button for the electric shock the moment his heart stopped—if it did.

Hopefully, the machine breathing for the guy would keep everything going. He straightened up and dropped the needle in the kidney dish. 'All done. How's that blood going, Jason?'

'It's good.'

'Rosie, what have you found?'

'I suspect the two bottom ribs below the wound on the left are fractured. There's also a second wound on the same side, nearer his back. Not deep. No blood loss.'

'Too busy being pumped out elsewhere.' Lucas looked around. 'Is Sandra still here seeing the woman with abdominal pain?'

'No,' someone answered. 'She went to grab a coffee about twenty minutes ago.'

'I'll get her to come and see to this man. Rosie, thanks for everything.'

Her smile was tired. 'I'm dismissed then?'

Inside, he went all soft. He totally understood that smile. He felt shattered too.

'You know we've got this now. Go while you can.' He had the phone in his hand. 'Get some sleep.' She looked as if she could drop off right where she was standing. 'I'll catch up later.' And climb into bed with her, hold her tight.

Rolling over onto her back, Rosie slowly opened her eyes and stared up at the ceiling. What had woken her? Had she inadvertently brought her phone in here when she'd dropped into bed when she'd got home from work? Normally, she left it in the kitchen after a difficult shift left her in dire need of sleep. Glancing at the bedside table, she couldn't see it.

The apartment bell rang. Who could want to see her? Her best friends both had family commitments this weekend, and Lucas had texted earlier to say he'd be round after he'd had some sleep, which had disappointed her. He could've slept with her, but then sleep would've been out of the question.

Crawling off the bed, she wrapped her satin robe around her and dragged her feet to the door. Pressing the buzzer, she said, 'Hello?'

No one answered. Someone must've pressed the wrong number.

A yawn gripped her. Coffee. Now that was what she needed in abundance. To wake up fully and feel a bit more energetic. Last night had been full-on, no rest between patients at all, and most of them had been tricky cases requiring all her focus for every moment she was with them. Working alongside Lucas with the stabbing victim had been intense and yet rewarding, with a better outcome than predicted.

Her jaw tightened at the thought of another incident of someone hurting others with no regard for what they were doing at all. How would they feel if it happened to them or their loved ones?

Just like that man had done to her in the car park, robbing and physically assaulting her all because he probably needed money for drugs. Even seeing a number of patients who'd been deliberately injured by others, it was only now, after she'd been attacked herself, did she really understand how it changed people's ability to wander around feeling one hundred percent safe. Most of the time she was fine, but there were instances when a sudden sharp noise had her leaping out of her skin and staring around, only to find no one approaching her looking threatening. It would take a while before she was completely comfortable out and about among strangers. Thankfully, the guy was going before the judge soon and then she could move on.

As the coffee brewed she picked up her phone to check for messages. Kelly suggested lunch tomorrow since Simone was out of town with her husband. No message from Lucas. Still asleep? She'd text him shortly and see if he felt like going to the pub later on. And if he said no? Then she'd be gutted. Better to carry on as though he hadn't got into her heart.

Slinging a pan on an element, she delved into the fridge for bacon and a couple of eggs. After that she'd get dressed and go to the mall for some retail therapy.

The doorbell buzzed again. What was going on? Was someone playing games with her? It had happened before when the guy one floor down had his son to stay and the kid went up and down the building ringing bells on every door and hiding before the door was opened. Or should she be nervous? No. She never used to be and she wasn't starting now just because of her assailant.

She pulled the door wide. 'What's going—' She drew to a halt, staring at Lucas, standing there looking so good she could almost eat him.

'Hello, Rosie. Have I come at a bad time?'

Heat filled her cheeks. 'Not at all. Come in.'

He held out a bunch of flowers she hadn't noticed. 'These are for you.' He followed that up with a terse laugh. 'Of course they are. Who else would I be bringing flowers for?'

Red roses. All bound together with a red and white ribbon and looking— 'Beautiful.' Burying her nose into the bunch, she breathed deep. 'My favourite scent.'

'It's become mine since we caught up.' Lucas smiled, sending her head into a spin.

She held the door wide. 'Coffee? Or bed first?'

Stepping inside, Lucas closed the door. 'I was going to suggest we go somewhere for a late lunch and let off steam about last night, and this morning's case. Like old times, even if it's only the two of us. But—' he caught her hand '—I've changed my mind. You had a better suggestion.'

'Good. I could do with an energy fix.'

'You want coffee?' He gave her a wicked grin.

'Later.' She turned for her bedroom, a small bounce in her step. Again, Lucas was the reason.

'Got a vase somewhere I can put these flowers into before you completely crush them?'

What? Rosie glanced down and blinked. The roses were squashed hard against her chest. 'Wonderful. Now look what I've done when you went to the trouble of bringing me flowers.' No one had ever done that before. This man was definitely a romantic, even if he had said they weren't getting into a long-term relationship. 'Lucas, the flowers are just gorgeous.'

His laugh was light and warm. 'Glad you like them. Where's a vase?'

Rosie relaxed. All was good here. It might not be quite how she wanted it, because she wasn't totally sure what that was yet, but she'd cope.

'In the cupboard under the bench. Meet you in the bedroom.'

CHAPTER EIGHT

Sitting on the deck of a restaurant overlooking St Kilda beach later that day, Lucas stretched his legs and leaned back in his chair after finishing some delicious fish and chips. 'Talk about perfect.' So was the company.

'Isn't it silly? I live in Melbourne but hardly ever come out here. It's not like it's difficult to get to.' Rosie was smiling non-stop, causing him to relax further. It was becoming his new normal. Should that worry him, or should he accept he was finally looking ahead, not backwards?

'Have you done anything about getting started on those flying lessons you were thinking about?'

'I talked to one of the instructors at the aero club out where I work. He said I can start any time I like, but I haven't had a lot of free time lately.' She laughed. 'Seems catching up with an old friend keeps me busy.'

He knew what she meant. Or thought he did. 'That might be the reason why I haven't got a lot of painting done either.'

'Don't blame me.'

'Of course I blame you. You're too big a distraction.'

More laughter, then her smile dimmed. 'Wonder how our girl with the back injury's getting on.'

Talk about deflating, but it was part of a doctor's life to think about cases at annoying moments.

'Her spinal X-ray confirmed a burst fracture in the mid back, so she had an MRI. It doesn't look like she'll be walking any time soon.' What a nightmare that had to be.

Rosie's hand covered his. 'Remember we always used to say no one knows what's ahead and we have to make the most of what we've got.'

Deep. Was Rosie implying that they should grab what they had and to hell with the consequences? Forget the short-term fling and go for the lot? If so, she had no idea how he could hurt her. Or be hurt himself. Though she did have a point. It was a reminder of how unpredictable life could be.

Rolling his hand over, he wrapped his fingers around Rosie's. 'I don't think I was very good at doing that.' He'd run away from his heartbreak rather than make a new life for himself.

'Back then, we didn't know how hard it might

be to do that. I think you've done well, but I've already told you that.'

The tension around his heart melted a little. 'Thanks.' It would be so easy to let Rosie in and let go of everything holding him back. Too easy, which had to be good, surely?

'It must be great living out this way.' Rosie was looking out at the beach.

He relaxed further into his chair. 'I agree.' Might be something to consider once he'd got his house up to spec. He shook his head. Rosie made everything seem uncomplicated and yet she had her own problems holding her back. She was also the one complicating his life right now— because he was letting her in and falling for her hard. Talk about messed up.

'What do you want to do after we leave here?' he asked as a diversion.

Rosie studied him for a moment. 'I'd like to see where you live and how you're getting on with the redecorating.'

He hadn't seen that coming, but it was fine. He had nothing to hide in that respect.

'No problem. Just warning you there's not a lot to see really. Just lots of paint tins and covers over the carpets in the lounge and dining room.'

'Still, I'll get to see what sort of place you like living in.'

'Remember I didn't buy the house on my own.

Unlike you and your apartment.' No compromises needed in Rosie's case.

'For me it was about deciding for myself. Growing up with Dad after Mum died was quite impersonal. No photos and all Mum's favourite ornaments were gone.' She paused, her finger rubbing a spot on the table top. 'Dad packed everything away the day after her funeral. When I asked if I could have some of the ornaments in my bedroom he said "no" and that was that. I don't know what happened to everything when he moved away. Probably went to the dump.'

'Blimey, Rosie, you must've been devastated.' He got up and went around to hug her. How could a father do that to his child? Lucas knew there was no way either of his parents would've been so harsh on him or Leon.

Rosie leaned into him for a moment, then pulled back. 'It's all right. I got used to it.'

Now he understood the blank spaces in her apartment, other than those two paintings. They'd stood out as exceptional for the emotions they'd evoked within him, and he suspected the same for anyone seeing them for the first time.

'Rosie, you're better than that. You're too lovely and kind to be anything but open-hearted. You've become your own person.'

Rosie stared at him. 'You think?'

She didn't?

'I know.' He took her hand and tugged her to her feet. 'Come on, let's go to my house so you can see who I am.' An ordinary guy who worried too much about his heart, and right now he was prepared to share it with this amazing woman who'd just let him in a little. He was more than ready to do this, come what may.

On the way back to Parkville, Rosie was quiet for a while, then she moved around on the seat so she was looking at him. 'I've not really talked about my parents very often to anyone except Kelly and Simone, and I've known them since school. Not that I've told you all that much either.'

'Rosie, the fact you said anything means a lot.'

Just as well he'd stopped for traffic lights as her smile was devastating as she responded to his comment. 'It does to me too.'

The lights changed and he pulled away with a jerk. 'Something to keep doing then—whenever you're up to it.'

Rosie was still watching him. 'I know I keep saying it, but I'm glad we've found each other.'

As in 'found each other' not as friends but lovers with a future? That sounded deeper than her usual casual way of wording things.

'I've had an insight into you as a doctor, and you haven't disappointed.'

'Changing the subject, by any chance?' She laughed. 'You're so damned grounded.'

'I figured you were ready for something light-hearted to talk about.'

'I thought I was the serious one, but I'm starting to understand that sometimes I can be flippant when I'm not overthinking things.'

'More like enjoying yourself. Flippant is the wrong word to describe you.'

Turning to face out of the windscreen, she laughed again. A wonderful sound that tripped his heart. It wasn't a sound he'd heard often from Rosie until recently, and that it came when they were alone together lifted his spirits further.

Looking up at the house Lucas had parked in front of, Rosie could only feel surprise.

'It's huge.' Nothing like she'd expected, though she didn't know why she'd thought that. Two storeys high, with wide verandas at the front and on the right-hand side, it made her apartment seem like a matchbox. A wide lawn swept down to the street. 'It must take hours to mow.'

'Not at all. I've got a ride-on.'

'Of course you have, being a man's man.' Slipping her arm through Lucas's, she said, 'Come on. I'm dying to see the rest.'

Inside the front door, she looked around. Wide stairs led up to the top floor. Doors opened off the entrance, showing spacious rooms with very little furniture.

'You haven't settled in fully by the looks of it.'

One eyebrow rose. 'I'm more interested in getting the place looking good at the moment. As I said, I don't even know if I want to carry on living here once I'm finished with redecorating.' He led her into what appeared to be the main lounge where there was a TV, stereo and two comfortable-looking lounge seats. 'I had intended putting on the second undercoat of paint this morning until I figured visiting you would be more fun. As it turned out to be.'

Warmth filled Rosie. They were getting on so well it was amazing. 'Definitely.' It was fulfilling too. She was falling deeper for him by the day. Scary as that was, she was okay. Lucas was worth the apprehension that sneaked in when she least expected it.

'Let's get the guided tour out of the way, then we can relax on the deck with a beer.' His grin was cheeky and told her more than anything that he also thought they were fine together.

'Lead on.' She took another look around the room. It seriously needed the paintwork done. 'You're going for a light colour with the top coat, I hope.' The windows didn't let in enough light for her.

'What would you use?'

'Dodging the question?'

'I'm interested in your opinion.' He picked up a paint chart. 'I'm using this light grey. It's already on the dining room walls and makes the room feel lighter and airier.'

'Good choice. It's very similar to what's on my walls.'

Would May have approved?

Gee, Rosie, stop that. May's gone. This is Lucas's house now.

True, but it was hard to deny that May had lived here with Lucas.

'Grey's in at the moment.' Lucas moved through to the kitchen with its wide bench where stools lined up on one side. 'No need to explain this space.'

'It's where you do most of your eating,' she noted. There was an empty mug and a plate with crumbs, along with a fishing journal and a book sitting on the counter.

'No point in setting a dining table. Here, I can make a mess, wipe it up and be done until next time. Except this morning I headed out the door to visit you instead.'

'I'm glad you did.' There it was. As simple as that. She enjoyed being with Lucas, wanted more time getting to know him better. One step at a time, she reminded herself as they headed upstairs, leaving thoughts of May on the ground floor.

At the top, Lucas spread his arms wide. 'Four bedrooms and two bathrooms, all very ordinary.'

That was it? He wasn't showing her the rooms? Think again, pal. Rosie stepped through the first door on her right, looked around and walked out again.

'Yes, it does need some loving attention.'

Lucas grinned and started along the hall to the next door. 'Same in here.' Then the next, 'And in here.' Then he turned around and led her back the way they'd come and past the top of the stairs. 'This is the first room I did up.'

The main bedroom. The room he'd shared with May. Her happiness slipped. She was in May's domain.

'What do you think?' Lucas asked.

Looking around, trying to deny what was going through her mind, she noted the room was light and cheerful with wide windows and co-lourful blinds and bedcovering. It would've been different before he'd decorated it. It was Lucas's room now. Nothing to do with May.

'Not bad.'

'It's the first time I've ever redecorated a room and I'm pleased with what I achieved.'

'You've done a great job.' The bed looked so inviting with the plump pillows and cosy duvet that Rosie had to turn away before she got too warm and bumped into Lucas. 'Oops.'

His hands were on her elbows, holding her lightly. His gaze was fixed on her like it did when they moved in on each other.

Anticipation caused her to shiver. 'Lucas?' His name was a whisper across her lips.

'I can't resist you.'

She couldn't pull away from him either. He was too desirable to turn her back on. She could get used to this. Wanted to get used to it. Winding her arms around his neck, she stretched up to kiss him.

Before her lips had covered his, she was being swung up against his chest and taken across the room, where he lowered her beside him as he knelt on top of the bed. 'You're certain?'

This time her mouth did cover his and she kissed him like there was no tomorrow. But there'd better be, she thought briefly as their bodies moved closer and their hands worked magic on each other. Tomorrow and beyond.

Rosie slowly opened her eyes to find Lucas watching her with a tender smile softening his sensual mouth. 'Wow,' she said on a slow exhale.

'Double wow.'

Their lovemaking only got better every time. She stretched her legs down the bed and rolled onto her side to face Lucas. Her body was loose and warm, and she felt cosy tucked up beside him. It was special. More special than she could recall from the past. She really was opening up to the possibility of a relationship. One she didn't walk away from when all the doubts and fears raised their heads, or was that getting too far ahead?

Normally, she protected herself by breaking things off when she got too close. While she and Lucas were supposed to be having a fling and no more, she did worry about hurting him. He'd been heartbroken when he'd lost May and didn't deserve to go through that pain again if he came to care for her and she walked away. She sighed. Talk about doing a U-turn with her fears. But hers were still there, right behind the worry about hurting Lucas.

'What was that sigh about?'

'It was my body saying thanks for such a wonderful moment or three.' She needed to cling onto that thought and stop letting her mind raise any number of reasons for not pursuing a relationship with Lucas.

'Moments? I need to work on that.' He rolled her on top of him and held her tight. 'But not right now.' He grinned. 'I haven't got my breath back completely.'

She'd been lying beside him for a while now. 'Your chest is barely rising,' she retorted and reached between them to touch his sex. 'You sure?'

'No.' His hands were on her backside, kneading softly.

Away we go again.

'Come on, then.'

'Turn around so I can wash your back,' Lucas instructed Rosie as they stood under the shower, letting the water stream over their tired bodies. Making out with Rosie was amazing, and he couldn't get enough of her. Except right now, he was exhausted in a wonderful kind of way. Not even standing here together could bring him fully to life at the moment. She'd sapped all his energy as she shared her body and left him feeling like he'd found himself again. An amazing sense of awareness filled him as he soaped her smooth skin between her shoulder blades and down to her trim waist. He was happy. Happier than he'd been in so long it seemed unreal. But it wasn't. The woman standing in front of him was all too real. He brushed his lips over her neck. 'You're lovely.'

Rosie turned around, and rubbed a lather over his chest. 'And you're wonderful. If you hadn't gone to the wedding with me, we probably wouldn't have got so close.'

'Or we still might have but it would've taken longer to get started.'

With her determination to be strong, despite what had happened to her after her assault, and then admitting she was struggling, she had got his attention straight away.

Her soft smile nudged his heart.

For him, sharing a shower with Rosie was intimate in a trusting way, as if they were exposing more about themselves than ever before. Nowhere to hide anything. Even the fear of being hurt again backed off in here. Either that or he was fooling himself because she was coming to mean so much to him. Yes, he cared a lot, maybe too much, for this beautiful woman and it was hard to imagine not going forward with her rather than taking a backward step into safety. Hell, he'd made love to Rosie in the room, the bed, that had been his and May's. It didn't distress him to think that, or make him feel guilty.

He was moving on.

Flicking off the shower, he stepped out and handed her a towel before taking his and drying off.

'Feel like a drink out the back on the deck?' Suddenly he needed to get out of this tiny space, put some air between him and Rosie. She was coming to mean too much if he could feel that May was slipping away.

'Sounds idyllic.'

He didn't know about idyllic, but it would be less stressful. He'd added the deck when he'd first returned home. It was his idea, his work, his place to wind down after difficult days and nights. He could comfortably share that with Rosie.

'So painting's definitely off the agenda for the rest of the day. Don't let me mess with your plans.' Her grin was mischievous, as though she'd be happy to watch him do some work while she lolled around with a drink in hand.

'It's totally your fault I haven't got anything done.' He wasn't making that up. It had been because he'd wanted to see her so badly that he'd gone around to her apartment earlier, and definitely she'd been the cause of his hard-on that had led to them making love.

'You're easily distracted.' She laughed. 'I like it.'

After winding the overhead sunshade out over the deck and getting some beers, he settled into a cane chair and stretched out his legs, his earlier tension dissipating as he chatted with Rosie. 'So, what do you think of my abode?'

'Honestly?'

'Is there any other way to answer?'

'It's not me, but that could be because it's in

need of the makeover you've started. There's a lot of space to be filled.'

'A family of six lived here when we bought the property.'

At the time, he and May had intended starting a family within a couple of years and then the rooms would've been filled with furniture, toys and clothes. Even when May had become fixated on climbing the corporate ladder, he'd still believed it was possible. He'd have been happy to be the primary stay-at-home parent until she'd established herself. What he hadn't understood was just how badly she'd wanted to get to the top of that ladder and what she was prepared to give up for it to happen. Now, he could admit that towards the end May hadn't been as focused on them as a couple as she had in the beginning.

'I can picture kids out here playing with a soccer ball or swimming in the pool.'

'Ahh, the pool that I haven't used once since I got back. It's a constant chore keeping it sparkling clean, let me tell you.'

'Why haven't you been in it when you've kept it so clean? I'd be in it every day if it was mine.'

He shrugged. 'No idea really. By the time I get home from work I'm more than happy to sit out here and contemplate my navel while I have a cold beer.'

Her laughter made him warm and happy. Happier. She just accepted him as he was. So good. Then a worrisome thought crossed his mind, shutting down the happy feeling. What if he did love Rosie? Would she love him back? Would he hurt her too at some point? Taking a long drink, he turned to look at the woman playing with his mind.

'What happened with you and Cameron? Everyone expected to be invited to the wedding.'

She didn't look shocked at the sudden question. 'I changed my mind.'

Lucas looked out across the lawn he'd once pictured his kids running around on and waited for more.

Finally, she continued. 'We talked about getting married but never did anything about it because I got cold feet. I hurt Cameron badly. And I hurt myself,' she added in a quieter voice.

'What changed your mind?'

'I wasn't ready.'

It didn't sound like the whole truth, which he'd like to know now that he was becoming emotionally invested in Rosie.

'But you'd been with him for a year and appeared happy.'

'I was, and then I wasn't. To have carried on would've been cruel to Cameron in the long run.' She upended her glass and drank a large mouthful, before looking at him with a tight smile.

'He's very happy now, with a lovely wife and a six-month-old daughter.'

'You keep in touch?' Seemed strange.

'Not at all. His wife, Brenda, used to work with a friend of mine in Sydney so I get the up-dates. Not that I particularly want them. It's over for me, and has been for a while.'

Did she mean she'd moved on and was ready for another relationship? Or was she pretending she was happy? No, he couldn't bring himself to believe that. When Rosie was happy, she was genuinely so. He'd go with the idea that she was ready for a new start. But then she did have is-sues about her father withdrawing from her. Did she carry those fears into other relationships? He longed to find out, but something held him back. He wanted to enjoy this time with Rosie, not stumble through his emotions with her and then have her walk away.

'Want to skinny-dip in the pool?'

'You a mind-reader? Though I'm not quite so keen on the naked aspect. Can any of your neighbours see into the yard?'

'I can't say for sure they can't. Want to bor-row one of my shirts? It would come halfway down your thighs.'

'I'm on.' She stood up. 'Come on, let's do this.'

Within minutes they were in the pool, Rosie swimming short lengths while he leaned against the side and enjoyed the view. That was until she came his way and sent a wave of water over his head. He dived under and grabbed her around the legs to pull her down.

Her hair floated behind her in a gorgeous mess and the shirt he'd lent her lifted up to her breasts and higher. She dived deeper, out of his hold, and headed for the end of the pool.

He followed, swimming as fast as possible, which wasn't fast enough to catch her.

'You're really good,' he spluttered when he caught up.

'Used to swim for my college.' She grinned. 'Definitely out of practice these days.'

'I'm learning more about you every day.' What was more, he was enjoying it. He *was* waking up to new possibilities. 'Things that have nothing to do with being a doctor.'

'You said you weren't sure about staying on here once you've got the house fixed up. Any further thoughts on that?'

Looking around the pool area, then at the back of the house, the answer came to him in a flash. 'I'm going to sell up and look for another property more to my liking.' It wasn't even a shock to find he'd made up his mind. It must've been lurking in the back of his head for a while and only now, being with Rosie, though she wasn't the reason for the decision, he knew what he was going to do. 'An up-to-date house with lots of light, open-space living and modern utilities.' He was ready to permanently put away this piece of his life.

'And a pool?' She grinned.

'Don't rush me into decisions I haven't thought about.' He returned her grin. 'It's taken nearly three months to get in this one.' But now he had, he'd keep going. Hopefully, he'd have Rosie's company as he did, although autumn was fast approaching so soon there wouldn't be a lot of swimming going on.

'I could do with a drink of water. All this exercise makes me thirsty. Want another beer?' She couldn't be thinking only of the minimal swimming she'd done. It had to be the lovemaking too.

'Sure do.' He climbed out of the pool and handed her one of the towels he'd brought outside. 'I'll turn the barbecue on to heat up while you're getting the drinks.'

'I'll check out your fridge and see what I can come up with for a salad.'

'You'll find most things you need, unless you're into exotic foods.'

'Not this girl.' She wriggled her butt and headed inside.

So easy being together when they weren't trying too hard to get along. Just as it had been during the weekend up north. He could get used to it all, he decided as he turned on the gas to bring the elements up to heat on the barbecue. Face it, he already was.

Rosie appeared, wearing the clothes she'd had on earlier, and carrying two bottles of beer. 'Here, get one of these into you.'

'I'm going to find some dry clothes first. The temperature's beginning to drop.'

'Hope there's not a storm brewing.' Rosie was checking out the skyline. 'Doesn't appear to be anything heading our way at the moment.'

'It should stay that way until we've had dinner. What's it like in the helicopter when there's a storm going on?'

'Most of the time it's not too bad, even quite exciting, but there have been instances where I'd have preferred to be on the ground. Of course the pilots won't fly if it's too rough, but we do get caught out occasionally.'

'I bet they hate pulling the plug on a flight if the patient is in serious trouble.' It'd be one of those decisions where they'd feel they couldn't win.

'They don't like it, but there's not a lot they can do other than be sensible and play safe. Right, I'll go make a salad.' She headed inside again, leaving her beer on the table. She was so relaxed in his place it was as though she'd been here often.

Smiling to himself, Lucas checked the barbecue and then went to put on dry clothes.

At his bedroom door he stopped and stared at the mussed-up bed, his smile growing. They had had the most amazing sex and he still could have more. Oh, yes, he was ready for more of everything. How long could a fling last before it became something deeper and long-lasting? Not too long, he hoped.

There was no mention of Rosie going back to her apartment. Instead, she followed him upstairs to his bedroom when they were done with dinner and cleaning up, and fell into his bed, reaching for him as though she'd been here often.

When she cuddled into him, her legs entwined with his after they'd made love long and slowly, he sighed with contentment. It seemed for ever since he'd had such a wonderful time.

CHAPTER NINE

'YOU WOULDN'T BE giving me a hard time about Lucas, would you?' Rosie sat on her deck with coffee in hand as she talked to Simone over the phone.

'Absolutely. The guy's gorgeous and he obviously thinks the same about you.'

'Shut up. You haven't got a clue what you're talking about.' Rosie grinned and rubbed her aching thighs. There'd been too much of a workout for her body over the weekend. Not that she regretted a single moment of her time with Lucas. They'd come a long way since they'd agreed to a fling. 'He's a friend from years ago, nothing more or less or—'

Or what? These days, he was a lot more than a friend. Where this was going was still a mystery, but one she was ready to try to unravel as fast as possible. On the good days she didn't want to miss out on anything, and the days when she feared she'd be let down by him were becoming fewer.

Simone laughed uproariously. 'It's about time you sounded flustered over a man. It's been for ever since one got under your skin and woke you up in a hurry.'

Rosie flushed. Her friend knew her too well.

'How's the sex?'

'Shut up,' she repeated as more heat spread through her.

'Bet you're blushing right now.'

'I'm going to get changed and go to the mall. I need some new walking shoes.'

What she needed to do was to hang up on Simone before she spilled about how she was falling in love with Lucas. It was too close to the truth to be able to keep it to herself much longer. Her friends had seen her go through breaking up with Cameron and had supported her all the way, even when she'd suspected they believed she'd made a mistake.

'Which mall are you thinking about? I'll meet you there in my lunch break.' Simone worked from home a lot and could take a break whenever she chose because she always made up the time and more.

Did she want to see Simone when her friend was teasing her so much?

'The usual.' It was near where Simone and Toby lived. 'I'm working tonight so won't be there all afternoon.'

'I'll see you around one.' Simone didn't hang up.

Rosie drew a breath. She had a feeling she knew what was coming, but couldn't find it in her to cut her friend off so she waited.

'Rosie, you really like Lucas, don't you?'

'Yes, I do.' Another breath and she continued. 'More than like him, if I'm honest.'

'I'm glad. Kelly and I have only met him once, but he came across as a great guy who'd always have your back. He had it that day after the assault. Throw in how you talk about him with so much happiness and enthusiasm and I think this guy might be a keeper.'

'Whoa, slow down. It hasn't been that long since we reconnected, and we're still getting to know each other in a deeper way than previously.'

Who was she trying to fool here? She wanted Lucas more than she'd ever have believed, and not only in bed.

'Don't put your usual walls up, Rosie. It's time to put yourself out there and take a chance on love.'

'You think I don't know that?'

'You know it all right. It's doing it that's your problem.'

Again, nothing she didn't already know and want to do something about, but what if she hurt Lucas? He didn't need that any more than she did.

'Shouldn't you be getting back to work?'

Simone sighed. 'Yes. I'll see you later. But please, please think of the future and not the past this time.' She hung up, leaving Rosie shaking her head.

And smiling. It was cool that her friend could be straightforward. There'd been a time when she wouldn't have let Simone get past the first sentence, but today she was grateful her friend had spoken her mind. Rosie drained her coffee. It seemed as though she might be finally letting go of some of her fears.

I'm ready for love and marriage and family.

She swallowed hard. Was she, really? Yes, she really was.

Time to get changed and go out. Sitting around the apartment gave her too much time to think about Lucas. There were worse things to think about, and nothing, no one, more exciting.

When she boarded the chopper for the first callout that night she wore a new pair of boots that she'd bought, along with walking shoes and a pair of heels to wear next time she and Lucas went out for a meal. There was also a new pair of jeans and a lightweight jersey in her wardrobe that she'd just had to have the moment she'd seen them.

Of course, Simone had given her a hard time

while enthusiastically going through the clothing racks looking for other clothes to tempt Rosie. After coffee and a snack, they'd spent nearly two hours going through the shops. So much for Simone getting back to work on time, but then she did say she'd been at the computer from seven that morning and deserved a long break.

Her phone rang as she buckled in. 'Lucas, I'll have to call you back later. We're about to lift off.'

'No problem. Any time. I'm not going anywhere.'

Shoving her phone in her pocket, she looked out of the window at the large hangar where the rescue helicopters were housed.

'You're looking pleased with yourself,' Dave said from the other seat.

Pleased? Definitely happy anyway. Life was exciting these days.

'I had a great three days off. How about you?' She didn't want him probing into what she'd been up to. There was only so much she'd talk about and Dave would be bored silly hearing about her shopping trip.

As Dave filled her in on his weekend she thought about Lucas and how staying at his house until late last night had been wonderful for the simplicity of it. She hadn't once felt she shouldn't be there or with him. A couple of times she'd wondered about how much Lucas had loved May, but it still felt right to be with him. Cooking meals together, talking, laughing, making love and going for walks with the neighbour's dog. It was a life without complications. She hadn't queried where she stood in Lucas's estimation, had accepted they were getting on great and left it at that. She'd never be as perfect as May, but she could live with that if Lucas could.

This sense of moving forward with her life was very new. Did the fact that she and Lucas had been friends first make it easier to trust her feelings for him? She'd seen him with May and knew he gave all he had when it came to a relationship. But the problem was *she* didn't. Though she did seem to be doing so this time.

'Five minutes to landing,' the pilot called.

Time to focus on work, not a certain man. Looking out and down, Rosie could see the flashing lights of police cars in the car park beside the beach, where a crowd had gathered. A young man had rolled his four-wheel bike on a sand dune and been crushed underneath the machine.

'Looks like they've lifted the bike off him.'

'Hope they had someone there with medical knowledge before doing that,' Dave said as the wheels touched down.

Unclipping her belt, she stood up and slung her pack over her shoulders. 'Me too.' She hadn't seen an ambulance in the parking area.

'Apparently the guy was racing up and down the dunes at a ridiculous speed,' Rosie told Lucas when they caught up later on the phone. 'No helmet either.'

'Makes you wonder what these people are thinking when they go out for a ride,' Lucas replied. 'Where'd you take him?'

'South Melbourne.' Parkville had been too far away when the case was so urgent. 'How was your day?'

'Much like any other, though without any heart-wrenching cases. I've been talking to a home decorator about getting the house finished. At the rate I'm going, it'll take till I retire to get it done.'

'So you're serious about selling and moving?' She'd wondered if he might change his mind when he thought about living there with May.

'I am. It's time. Not that I've spent a lot of time here since May died, but this place is part of a different life.'

Wow. These days, Lucas could talk about his past in small bites without hesitating. He *was* moving forward.

'Any idea where you might move to?'

'Not yet. I'll leave that for now.'

'I had a phone call today from Megan, the cop. She told me the guy who assaulted me is going before the judge on Friday and if I wanted to go along I could.'

'It might give you some closure. I'll go with you, if you like.'

No surprise there.

'Thanks, Lucas. You always have my back, don't you?'

'I try. Think about it and let me know what you decide.'

'I'm going. I want to face him, show I'm not a blithering mess because of him.'

'That's my Rosie.'

Her heart warmed. His Rosie. She loved it, loved Lucas. She did? Yes, she did. Not that she was quite ready to put it out there though. The fear of being rejected hadn't completely disappeared. Would it ever? Damn, she hoped so, or life ahead looked lonely.

Dave appeared in the doorway. 'We're on.'

'Sorry, Lucas, I've got to go. Talk tomorrow.' It was after eleven and he'd probably head to bed soon.

She really loved Lucas? Yes, for better or worse, she did.

'Take care.'

'I will.' Now she had someone to spend her free time with she'd be ultra careful. A sudden image of her assailant filled her head, those wide staring eyes and ugly grin reminding her that being safe wasn't as easy as she'd once believed, but she was prepared to face him. *And* she'd have Lucas with her while she did.

It was the night before Rosie was going to court to hear the judge sentence her assailant and Lucas had kept her company all day in an attempt to take her mind off tomorrow.

She was grinning in that way that always tightened his gut, and his crotch. 'We're together a lot of the time outside work, so I guess it doesn't matter that I don't come to your department often. I have been there twice in the last two weeks. There are some other nice doctors working there.'

'Nice? I'm nice?' He leaned in and kissed her cheek. 'Try again.'

'Okay, you're sexy whereas they're not.'

'Phew.' Not that he felt he'd let her down in that department.

They were sprawled over her bed after mind-blowing sex. They'd spent most of the day at Phillip Island, where they'd walked the beach and ate fish and chips, trying not to get sand in the food. Returning to the city, he'd come up to her apartment and here they were, sated and relaxed. Being with Rosie got better by the day.

Rosie got off the bed and headed to her en suite bathroom. 'I'm going to grab a shower and then throw something together for dinner.'

Should prove interesting as there wasn't much in her fridge. When he joined her out in the kitchen after his shower, he couldn't smell anything. 'What are you making?'

Handing him a beer, she said, 'Seafood pizza.'

'Put together by the outlet down the road?'

'That's the one.' After pouring herself a wine, she wandered through to the lounge and stood staring at one of the paintings that had stirred him deeply the first time he'd seen them.

Moving up beside Rosie, he took in the brilliant colours and soft shapes of the outback setting. Once again, he was drawn in and could feel his heart beating a little faster.

'Have you ever been to the Outback?'

'No.'

'What did your father do out there?'

'Opal mining. When he died, I learned he'd worked on his own, miles from anyone, which is dangerous. He had a heart attack and might've been saved if he hadn't been alone.' Rosie took a mouthful of wine and turned to him. 'Dad became a complete loner after Mum died.'

Now he was beginning to understand even more about what made Rosie tick. It would be a big hurdle to get over if they were to have a future together. He waited.

Rosie paced across the room, then turned to face him. 'The day Mum passed, Dad withdrew from everything and everyone. It was as though he'd died too. Johnno and I never went without any of the basics. We were well fed, clothed and housed. Our university fees were paid for, as was anything we required. But…' her chest rose high, dropped low '…he never again showed us love. Up until then, he'd been as loving a father as any kid could wish for. It was as though he was afraid to love us in case we were lost to him too.'

Lucas struggled to keep from hugging her, to hold her close and comfort her, but he sensed it would be the wrong thing to do. Rosie had said she never talked about her father and now that she was the last thing she'd want would be sympathy.

'I can't imagine what you both went through.' Were still going though, by the sound of it. His parents had never backed off from him or Leon, were still always there whenever they might be needed.

'Be thankful you can't.' Bitterness laced her words. Then she glanced back at the paintings. 'Yet I question his feelings because of these paintings. He created them and left them to us. They have our names on the back. He always made sure we never went without a thing. Yet when I left home to go to university he was quick to head away. As far as I know, he never returned home. He missed both our graduations and Johnno's first wedding.'

What a mixed-up man he must've been.

'It's hard to understand what was going on inside his head. Obviously, he adored your mother.'

'Too much if he could do what he did.' Rosie moved to sit down.

Joining her, Lucas reached for her hand, held it on his thigh. 'You've done well, despite everything.'

Tugging her hand away, she shuffled around to face him full-on. 'Have I? When I struggle to get close to anyone, to trust a man with my heart? I've never been able to, and sometimes I doubt I ever will.'

His heart hit the ground. She was hurting now. Telling him what had gone on in her past was causing her pain. He didn't want that. She was also warning him to be aware of what she could do to him, how she could hurt him.

'You're better than that. I've seen you with Simone and Kelly, with Johnno. Your smiles are soft and loving, your eyes shine. You *do* let others in.' He drew a breath and put it out there. 'You're the same with me. I don't ever feel as though you're worried I might let you down.'

'You don't understand, Lucas. I'm afraid to open up entirely, afraid of being hurt, not just by friends but by any partner I might have.'

That explained why she'd called off her relationship with Cameron. She'd been afraid he'd leave her.

'Do you think you look for problems that aren't there when you're in a relationship?'

'I have to protect myself.'

In other words, yes. That was scary. Perhaps he should explain where he was at with May the night she'd died.

'May and I had an awesome marriage, were very happy together.'

'I know. It was obvious all the time.'

Not behind the scenes, it wasn't.

'Actually, things were already changing. We were beginning to argue a lot. May was moving to Sydney, whether I agreed to it or not. I would've moved if she'd talked it through with me instead of saying that's what we were doing or she'd just go on her own, without me.'

Rosie's eyes widened. 'Truly? That's not how it goes in a relationship. Not how I'd approach it anyway.'

Sadness touched him. 'Me either. Nor would May in the beginning. She seemed to get caught up in making it to the top of the corporate ladder to the extent that nothing else mattered, including our marriage.'

Rosie's hand was warm on top of his. 'I would never have guessed you were going through that. You always seemed so happy with her.'

Go on. Tell her everything then there'd be no comeback if they continued this relationship. That was a big *if* since she'd warned him she got spooked easily and wasn't great at staying around.

'What I'm saying is that there's always risk in any relationship, no matter how loving it starts out. Looking back, I think my love for May had already begun to fade a little, and I'm certain hers had for me. I was no longer as important as her career and I probably locked down a little and made things worse. There were other problems too. We'd always talked about the kids we'd have, then she changed her mind about wanting a family, said they'd get in the way of her career, which isn't what she'd said when we first got married.'

'You must have felt guilty over the accident that took her life.'

'I still do. We argued again on the phone that night about me not being able to celebrate her promotion with her, but if I'd gone home instead of helping a critically ill patient...' He paused, started again. 'There are a lot of ifs. Basically, I should've been patient and waited till we were together to celebrate her promotion and then talked about what we were doing next. I didn't. I was angry with May for saying she didn't want children any more, and that we were moving, whether I liked it or not, and I just pulled away.'

Rosie was staring at him as if something was wrong.

'What's up?'

'Nothing.'

'Come on, Rosie. There is, and you know it. Don't hold out on me, whatever you do.'

Like May used to. Oh, no. No, no, no. This couldn't be right. Rosie was not May. He'd loved May with all he had. He was falling deeply for Rosie, but he struggled to understand his feelings at the moment. Maybe he was there. And now he'd shown Rosie he could withdraw from the woman he'd loved more than life, and she was always on the lookout for that exact thing happening to her. Basically, he'd put a big warning sign on his forehead.

Watch out. I'm not to be trusted.

He reached for her hands. He needed to explain how he felt, to show he could be trusted. He loved her. But he'd failed last time with May, so she'd think there wouldn't be any guarantees that his love could last for ever. Did anyone have those? He didn't think so.

Pulling back before he could say a word, she said, 'I need time to think about what you've told me.'

'Talk to me. Ask whatever you want to know.'

'I don't need to. I get the picture, as clear as can be.'

Clunk. A dart hit his heart. She was seeing the worst of him, not the best. He wanted to fight back, explain how he'd changed and wouldn't repeat his mistakes, but her face was closed off, her body erect and tight. The barriers were in place.

'Rosie, you can trust me.'

She stared at him. There was a high chance she'd walk away, unable to love him because of her fear of being discarded. 'You should go now.'

He said quietly, 'I mean it, Rosie.' Even though she'd told him to go he had to stay or she'd believe she was right about how he could walk out of her life.

Pain filled Rosie's face as she snapped at him. 'This is the first time I've ever let a man get so close to me, let him into my heart, and you're doing exactly what I was afraid of. Walking away.'

'I'm not walking away. I never said that. *You* asked *me* to leave.'

Maybe he had to go so she had time to calm down and think it all through.

'I've spent my whole adult life looking for love and walking away before it could happen, and now when I want to take a chance, look what happens. You tell me you weren't as happy with May as I believed…that you were arguing all the time and by the end your marriage was just a sham. That you locked down, pulled away from her.'

He froze at the despair in her voice. 'I was telling you the truth about what happened, not hiding it.' His mouth was dry. 'May and I had a terrific relationship but we met when we were eighteen and I think, as we grew older, we wanted different things from our lives.' That was the conclusion he'd finally come to. 'Whereas you and I are adults and established in our careers and it's time for more—together.'

She winced at his honesty. Not used to it from the men she got close to? Or looking for more problems?

'You mean the world to me, Rosie.'

'You can have whatever future you want without me, because I'm not risking getting hurt. I cannot commit to you, knowing this. I can't face being dumped by you in the long run, because I don't believe in myself. I tried before and had to get out. I'm totally messed up, Lucas, and I know it. I'm so sorry but we're done. Please go now.'

For a long moment he watched her, now fully

understanding just how much he loved her and just how hurt she'd been by her father's actions. But to tell her how he felt would bring another verbal dart to his heart. She wouldn't believe him.

Heading for the door, he could feel his heart sinking lower and lower with every step he took. It felt as if he was leaving Rosie for good. Which he probably was.

''Bye, Rosie.'

Silence followed him out of the door, which he closed carefully behind him.

'I love her,' he murmured to himself. 'I'll be back. She needs me beside her, backing her. Showing her she can trust me and let my love in.'

Wrapping her arms around herself, Rosie held on tight in an attempt to prevent herself from falling into little pieces. Lucas had gone. As she'd told him to. What had happened there? They'd been sharing their pasts and then suddenly it had become tense and awkward.

Lucas saying he'd started to fall out of love with May had shocked her to the core. He was the one man who she'd always believed had committed to one woman for ever. Of course she was being naïve. Not all relationships lasted for ever. It was a dream to believe that.

Not all parents loved their kids unconditionally or for ever either. Was she bitter or what? Bitter or covering her resentment that her father hadn't loved her enough to be part of her life in all aspects? She'd resented him hugely for withdrawing from her and Johnno. So why had she done the same thing to Cameron when she'd known he'd loved her? Why do it to Lucas before she'd really given them a chance? Because he'd got too close to her fear when he'd talked about May and how he hadn't loved her as much towards the end. In showing his vulnerability he'd cranked up hers, sending her instantly into self-protection mode.

Staring sightlessly out of the window, she could feel her heart splintering. Yes, she had fallen in love with Lucas when she hadn't been looking. Believing he was only a friend had made it too easy to pretend nothing was going on in her heart. But she did love the man. More than she'd ever have believed possible. To the point she'd stick by him and push all her doubts aside, come what may?

More than anything, she wanted to believe she would. That she could. But old habits didn't just go away because she wanted them to. Loving Lucas didn't mean she could instantly let go of all her fears. But she should because he always had her back, and he *wouldn't* let her down. It was hard to believe he thought he might not have loved May as much towards the end. There'd been no sign of that years ago. Guess it wasn't something to be put out there for everyone to see though.

Her phone rang.

Go away, whoever you are.

It might be Lucas.

So?

So she wanted to hear his voice.

I can't talk to him.

Crossing to get her phone, she stared at the screen.

Kelly.

No way was she answering. Kelly knew her too well to believe she was fine and having her girlfriends dropping by tonight was the last thing she needed. Time alone thinking about Lucas mightn't be best either, but it was what she'd do. Face it, she wasn't about to fall asleep the moment she climbed back into her messed-up bed with all its memories of making love with Lucas.

The doorbell clanged.

What now? Had Lucas returned to tell her he wanted to be a part of her life?

Hauling the door wide, she stared at the teenager holding two pizza boxes. Dinner. Not Lucas. She needed to pay the kid.

'Just a moment.' Her mind was a blank. Where had she left her bag?

The teenager held the boxes out to her. 'It's all right. A man paid me at the main door and then let me in to come up.'

Lucas. Had to be. Who else would do that?

'Thanks.' She had no idea if she was thanking the teenager or Lucas. Closing the door, she took the pizzas to the kitchen and dropped them on the bench. Her appetite had long vanished, along with Lucas.

At home, Lucas tossed his shoes into the wardrobe and threw himself on the bed to stare up at the ceiling. What had happened at Rosie's? For a moment there he'd thought they were making progress and Rosie understood him so he could stop worrying about letting her down if they got into a deeper relationship. Then he'd admitted to the problems he'd had with May in their marriage and that had been like proving to Rosie that he wasn't to be trusted to stay around for ever, even if he loved her.

'I do love her.' He loved everything about Rosie. She was amazing and special and beautiful and tough. The list was endless. Then tonight he'd gone and blown it. Rosie was never going to abandon her fear of rejection, even if he managed to sneak into her heart.

Just because he had fallen for her didn't mean his feelings were reciprocated. Yet she always gave herself completely. Like when they made love. Yes, they made love, they didn't just have sex. It had always been special with Rosie. She was one incredible woman who he adored. Totally and utterly.

So why was he here and not at her apartment telling her this?

Not because she'd told him to go but because he was an idiot. When the going got tough he'd backed off fast. Because he'd told himself he had to protect Rosie by giving her space, but in reality, he was also protecting himself. The guilt over not being there for May when she'd been thrilled with her promotion and wanted to celebrate with him was real, but it had diminished over the years since. He couldn't hold onto it for ever as an excuse not to step out and try again to have love and a family. No one wanted to have their heart broken, but to have loved and lost was far better than not to have tried at all.

He'd told Rosie about him and May because he knew he loved her now. She hadn't seen that he'd never deliberately let her down. Life threw curve balls for sure, but they could talk through those together. They had to. Did Rosie care about him at all? He was certain she did. Did that mean she loved him? He wasn't so sure, but he wasn't going to find out unless he fronted up and laid his heart on the line.

Which he would do. Decision made. He had nothing to lose and a lot to gain. Sitting up, he checked his phone. One a.m. Okay, not the best time to turn up at Rosie's door and ask to be let in. He had to wait till the sun came up around seven. What to do in the meantime? Sleep was out of the question. Impossible with how his mind wouldn't shut down. Rosie this, Rosie that. Damn, but she'd got to him in a big way. A way he did not want to give up. He loved her, as simple as that.

Then he remembered the creep was appearing before the judge in the morning and he knew immediately what he was going to do.

Rosie rolled over and buried her face in the pillow. What was she supposed to do with herself until she went to court to see the man who'd messed with her get his sentence? Call in and see if there was any work she could do? Yeah, and have Steve give her a hard time about not having a life outside her job. Maybe she didn't. No way. She did, and it centred round Lucas.

Because he was everything to her. And she'd let him walk out of here last night. They both needed to think about things, he'd said, and she'd agreed. What had she been thinking? She hadn't been. That was the problem. Other than for reasons to keep Lucas at a distance, which really was the last thing she wanted. She loved him. End of. No, not that. It wasn't an ending. It was the beginning of something special—if she had the guts to tell him how she felt. Why wouldn't she if it meant finding what she'd been looking for most of her life?

Groaning, she hauled herself out of bed and went to stand under the shower until the water ran cold. Then she went through her wardrobe to find an outfit that was serious without being boring. A navy trouser suit was the best on offer. Adding a red blouse to the mix lifted the dark blue and added colour to her pale face.

Lucas had said he'd go with her to the sentencing. After last night she had no idea what he intended doing. She wasn't phoning him to find out. It was his decision to make and not one she wanted to influence. If he cared for her as much as he'd indicated then he'd be there. He'd have her back as he had other times, and hopefully today would be no different. It might be the game changer she needed if he turned up.

Or she might be a fool even thinking like this. For all she knew, he might've walked out of here for the last time, never to come back and enjoy sitting on the deck, sharing a wine and talking about their day.

She was such an idiot for letting him go. For kicking him out of her apartment. She should've reached out and told him how she felt about him, said she loved him and was still afraid but willing to do anything in her power to be worthy of him.

I do love you, Lucas.

If nothing else had come from last night, that had. It was the truth, and she was ready to step up and show him how much. Ready to put all her fears aside and have a wonderful life in love with Lucas. To stop doubting herself and finally have that happy life she craved.

She glanced at the watch on her wrist. It had been her mother's and she wore it most days. Blink. What was going on? Had it stopped? Less than an hour had passed since she'd crawled out of bed. How was she going to fill in the hours till she went into the courtroom?

Go see Lucas.

He wasn't home when she tentatively pushed the doorbell. Her heart skipped a couple of beats as her mind came up with a dozen reasons for that. He'd got called into work, was out walking the neighbour's dog, had gone to the supermarket, gone around to see her and she wasn't there.

Swiping at the tears slipping out of the corners of her eyes, she turned around and headed back the way she'd come. Lucas wasn't at her apartment. Her heart dropped further. She'd been crazy to think he might've been.

She couldn't stay around here wondering if she'd ever get a chance to tell Lucas how she felt. Might as well head into the city early.

Other than lawyers, there weren't many people in the courtroom when Rosie sank onto a seat near the front. Looking around, she shivered. This was where people's lives were decided upon with little input from themselves. It was nothing like how she'd got to where she was, becoming a doctor because she'd wanted to and prepared to work hard to get there. Mind you, the man who'd attacked her had made a decision to do that to her, and deserved whatever punishment he got. Hopefully, the judge wouldn't be too soft on her assailant.

A court official stood up. 'Call Gerald Black-more to the stand.'

A guard led a man in, handcuffed to his wrist.

Rosie gasped. That was the man, right there, looking almost pathetic now he wasn't drugged to the eyeballs and leering at her.

'You okay?' Lucas sat down beside her and reached for her hand.

'I am now.' Her heart was beating erratically and she didn't think it had anything to do with Gerald Blackmore.

'He's quite disappointing, isn't he?' Lucas said quietly.

Damn it, she was smiling. 'Very.'

Lucas was here—with her. What more did she need?

'He's looking this way.'

Rosie sat up straighter and stared back at the man who'd attacked her. He wasn't going to undermine her strength again.

The smirk on his face faded and he looked down at his feet.

Lucas squeezed her hand. 'Go you.'

Glancing at her man, she beamed at him. 'I'm tough when you're with me.'

A gavel banged, interrupting her happy moment, and for the next few minutes they listened to the judge comment on Blackmore's crimes before sentencing him to two years behind bars.

Outside on the footpath, Lucas took Rosie in his arms. 'How does that make you feel?'

'Two years doesn't seem long enough, but it's better than a slap on the hand, I guess.' She was smiling. 'Lucas, I have to tell you something.'

'Let's go somewhere less busy.' It was lunchtime and there were crowds heading in all directions around them.

'To heck with private. I want the whole world to know I love you, Lucas. With all my heart, I love you, and I'm sorry about last night.'

He stared at her as hope and excitement flared,

and grew into wonder. 'Me too.' Shaking his head, he tried again. 'Last night was a mess. It probably had to be got out of the way, but I'm sorry for how it went down. I love you too. My heart is yours to keep.'

The wonder in Rosie's face had him pulling her in for a hug that quickly became a kiss that even the elbow-knocks from passers-by didn't detract from.

When they came up for air, Rosie was beaming. 'I won't walk away, Lucas. This is for real and I can't imagine not having you at my side for ever.'

'I won't change my mind about how much I love you either, unless it grows even more.' Without another thought, he dropped to his knee and took her hands in his. 'Marry me, Rosie, and make me the happiest man on the planet.'

Leaning down, she brushed a sensational kiss on his mouth. 'Try stopping me. That's a yes, in case you're wondering.'

He stood up and swung her up in his arms. 'Let's go celebrate, my darling. And start planning a wedding.'

'I already know where I want to go for that.'

'The place we got together.'

'I'm not getting married in an emergency department.' She grinned.

'How about the same vineyard in the Yarra

Valley where Johnno and Karen tied the knot?'
He grinned back.

'You read my mind.'

EPILOGUE

Five months later

Lucas stopped breathing as he stared at the beautiful woman watching him as she walked towards him with the biggest smile ever. She held a large bouquet of red roses and wore a white wedding dress that highlighted her stunning body as it flowed out behind her. His heart lifted.

Rosie.

Her brother had her arm tucked firmly in his and looked happy for her, which gave *him* a sense of relief. He'd hate to get on the wrong side of Johnno. But the guy was with his sister for this special occasion, and standing up with him and Leon afterwards. He guessed that meant he'd made the grade.

Rosie.

They were getting married, were committing to for ever, and making him the happiest man possible. His heart was in a frenzy, beat-

ing madly while his mouth was dry and his head
light.

Rosie.

She was all he wanted, needed and loved.

Rosie.

She looked to him as she and Johnno reached
the end of the aisle, her smile so wide and open
and loving that Lucas felt his heart squeeze,
something it did a lot these days.

Life couldn't get any better than this.

The marriage celebrant cleared her throat.
'Let's get you two married, shall we?'

Karen's mother, Sheree, had offered to marry
them when she'd heard about the wedding and
they'd both been more than happy to accept.

'Karen's family is mine now too,' Rosie had
said at the time.

Now she grinned. 'Bring it on.'

'Take it slowly, enjoy the moment.' Sheree
laughed. 'This only happens once so you've got
to make some special memories.'

Lucas was certain his head was already full
of those. Seeing Rosie in her stunning gown
and holding her favourite flowers had torn at
his heart, tightened his gut and made him happier than ever. If that was possible.

Sheree became serious. 'Lucas Tanner, do you
promise to love Rosie for ever, to protect her and
care for her, be the best partner for her?'

'Absolutely I do. I will always love you, Rosie.' He hadn't kept to the short script, but hey, this was his marriage ceremony.

'Rosie Carter, do you promise to love Lucas for ever, to have his back and care for him, be the best partner for him?'

'I do with all my heart.' Rosie stretched up and brushed a kiss on his chin.

'Hang on, you two. We're not quite done yet,' Sheree admonished through a big smile. 'Leon, have you got the wedding rings?'

'Lucas would have my hide if I didn't.' Leon grinned as he took a ring box from his pocket.

Lucas took the etched gold band from the box and turned to Rosie. 'This ring marks my dedication and love to you.' He slid it over her finger and kissed the back of her hand. Nearly there.

A tear trickled from the corner of Rosie's eye. This was the best day of her life. Never had she believed she'd get here and feel so completely relaxed about handing her heart over in front of family and friends, knowing she'd never get cold feet.

'Rosie?' Sheree said quietly. 'Your turn.'

She blinked, grinned. 'Just making the most of the moment, making those memories you mentioned.'

Kelly and Simone laughed beside her.

Reaching for the other ring, she took Lucas's hand in hers. 'Lucas, with this ring I give you my heart for ever.' Then she slid the ring in place and stretched up to kiss him lightly.

As their families and friends applauded and called congratulations, she leaned in close, still grinning, and said quietly, 'There's more. I'm two months pregnant.'

His head jerked upward and his eyes widened as a stunned smile appeared, and grew and grew. 'And I thought things couldn't get any better.'

She kissed him. 'Shows you don't always get it right.' But he had been right in loving her and making her dreams come true. 'I love you, Lucas Tanner.'

'Back at you, Rosie Tanner.'

* * * * *

If you enjoyed this story,
check out these other great reads
from Sue MacKay

Brooding Vet for the Wallflower
Healing the Single Dad Surgeon
Paramedic's Fling to Forever
Marriage Reunion for the Island Doc

All available now!

HARLEQUIN
Reader Service

Enjoyed your book?

Try the perfect subscription for Romance readers and get more great books like this delivered right to your door.

See why over 10+ million readers have tried Harlequin Reader Service.

Start with a Free Welcome Collection with free books and a gift—valued over $20.

Choose any series in print or ebook.
See website for details and order today:

TryReaderService.com/subscriptions

RSBPA24R